She *Had* To Surface From Under His Spell…

"Now that we've gotten the dinner you've been harping on for years out of the way, I hope we can discuss something important." As Clarissa spoke, Ferruccio's eyes drained of the warmth that had ignited them for the past hours. She braced herself against the urge to soften her tone. "So…go ahead. Negotiate. I can't wait to hear your 'terms.' They should be entertaining."

After the shock passed, rage crashed over Ferruccio. How had she blindsided him again? He could swear she'd taken off her mask and shown him her true self. Now she'd thrown his invitations in his face, taunted him. It didn't matter that he would be king. He remained a bastard in her eyes.

She had no idea who she was dealing with, how out of her depth she was. It was time to make her regret her snobbery.

"You want to negotiate, Princess? By all means. I have only one term for agreeing to take the crown. That I take you with it."

Dear Reader,

As I wrote the last words in *The Illegitimate King,* the book that wraps up THE CASTALDINI CROWN trilogy, I found myself sighing in pleasure and regret. To have come to the satisfying end of a family saga that has been all I thought about for five months made me feel at once elated and wistful. I've fallen in love with each of my magnificent heroes. It was as wonderful to have known them as it was hard to leave them behind.

Then I remembered that I can always open the books and revisit them, and that I can and will create more one-woman men who are everything a woman might dream of. Men who are powerful in character and passion as well as in sensitivity, who are towers of strength and tenderness at once.

The Illegitimate King's hero, Ferruccio Selvaggio, aka the Savage Iron Man, is such a man, but he surprised even me as I wrote his story. He was bent on revenge, but the side of him that longed for love and family overwhelmed his harsh intentions at every turn. I loved him that tiny bit more for having triumphed over unimaginable horrors and hardships to become the incredible man who would become Castaldini's king, and the one man his heroine, Clarissa, could love.

I hope that reading their story will give you as much pleasure as writing it gave me.

I would love to hear from you at oliviagates@gmail.com.

You can also visit me on the Web at www.oliviagates.com.

Thank you for reading.

Olivia Gates

THE ILLEGITIMATE KING

OLIVIA GATES

Published by Silhouette Books
America's Publisher of Contemporary Romance

Recycling programs for this product may not exist in your area.

ISBN-13: 978-0-373-76954-4

THE ILLEGITIMATE KING

This edition published by arrangement with Harlequin Books S.A.

Visit Silhouette Books at www.eHarlequin.com

Printed in U.S.A.

Books by Olivia Gates

Silhouette Desire

**The Desert Lord's Baby* #1872
**The Desert Lord's Bride* #1884
**The Desert King* #1896
†The Once and Future Prince #1942
†The Prodigal Prince's Seduction #1984
†The Illegitimate King #1954

*Throne of Judar
†The Castaldini Crown

OLIVIA GATES

has always pursued creative passions—painting, singing and many handcrafts. She still does, but only one of her passions grew gratifying enough, consuming enough, to become an ongoing career: writing.

She is most fulfilled when she is creating worlds and conflicts for her characters, then exploring and untangling them bit by bit, sharing her protagonists' every heart-wrenching heartache and hope, their every heart-pounding doubt and trial, until she leads them to an indisputably earned and gloriously satisfying happy ending.

When she's not writing, she is a doctor, a wife to her own alpha male and a mother to one brilliant girl and one demanding Angora cat. Visit Olivia at www.oliviagates.com.

At the end of this trilogy, I again dedicate it to
the two ladies who made it possible for me to write it.

My phenomenal editor, Natashya Wilson.

And Melissa Jeglinski, a wonderful lady
and Desire's former senior editor.

Thanks, ladies. It's been a fantastic ride.

Prologue

Six years ago

"So gods *do* walk the earth!"

Clarissa D'Agostino frowned at her friend's breathless exclamation as she dabbed at the stain on the décolleté of her lavender chiffon gown.

She cursed herself for biting into that overripe plum. Way to go, making a fool of herself when she was supposed to be Castaldini's princess, all grown up and fit for court appearances at last. It seemed that four years in the States and graduating at the top of her class from Harvard Business School hadn't done a thing to improve her ability to handle public appearances.

She grimaced at the visible stain. "What are you going on about?"

"I'm all about that…*god* over there!"

Clarissa swung around. Not to search out the proclaimed deity, but to check her best friend for signs of intoxication.

She found Luci fanning herself. "And I thought his profile was hard-hitting. His full-frontal assault is devastating."

Clarissa gaped at her. Luciana Montgomery, whose feminist outlook and American side dominated her Castaldinian roots, was the last woman she knew who'd drool over a man. She'd never seen Luci react like this to anyone—not in the States, where they'd gone to college together and where hunks had regularly pursued the vivacious redhead, and not in Castaldini, which was crawling with gorgeous men. The only men Luci had ever even said were drool-worthy were Clarissa's brothers and a few of her cousins. And she hadn't reacted this way to any of them. It was weird, seeing her tongue almost lolling out.

The weirdness took a turn into the absurd when Luci grabbed her arm and squeaked in excitement, "He's looking our way!"

"I could have sworn you had only one glass of champagne, Luci." Clarissa turned to investigate the phenomenon who had made the most poised twenty-two-year-old woman she knew flutter like a giddy schoolgirl. "I'll have to see if someone's spiking the…"

The words backed up in her throat.

There were so many men in the ballroom whom Clarissa didn't recognize. She'd been away for so long and had never been active in court life, and she was the one member of the king's family who everyone almost forgot existed, just the way she wanted them to. But there could be only one man who warranted Luci's overreaction.

There was only one man who Clarissa could see.

He wasn't a god. He surpassed all depictions of gods she'd ever seen, with all the perfections worshippers' imaginations had lavished on them. No one could have imagined *him.* She certainly hadn't. She could barely believe he was real.

He was. And he *was* looking their way. *Her* way.

Her heart plunged into the pit of her stomach. Time ceased. Reality fell away. Existence converged onto one thing. His eyes. Stormy skies illuminated by lightning, all their focus and power targeting her. But what started tremors arcing through her was what she saw in them; a reflection of her own state, stunned free fall into the awareness that crackled between them.

Suddenly he blinked, turned his face away. Through the fugue encompassing her, she realized why he had severed their connection. Her father.

King Benedetto had appeared beside the man, a wide smile—one she couldn't remember seeing since she was a small child—spreading across his lips.

The man gazed at her father as if he didn't recognize him. Her father spoke, the man listened. She found herself moving, unaware of anything or anyone, just needing to be closer, to find out what had just happened. Suddenly the man turned back, snared her again in the bull's eye of his focus.

She stopped. Moving. Breathing. Her heart quivered inside her to a standstill. Shock splashed through her like ice water.

It was unmistakable, what she saw in his eyes now. Coldness. Hostility. Which meant one thing. She'd been wrong. It hadn't been a blast of attraction she'd seen in his eyes, felt radiating from him. That had all been on her side.

Before she could recoil from the rush of mortification and letdown, he turned and walked away from her father.

She stood there, feeling as if a knife had been thrust between her ribs, heard Luci's voice as if it were seeping in from another realm.

"Lord, what was *that?*"

Clarissa couldn't produce a thought, let alone an answer.

"*That* was the Savage Iron Man."

Clarissa swung around unsteadily toward the purring voice.

Stella. She'd been making Clarissa's skin crawl ever since they were children. Thankfully, they were only third cousins, so she'd seen as little of Stella as possible. She would have liked to see far less. None.

Stella's words made as much sense now.

It was Luci who summed up Clarissa's thoughts: "Huh?"

"Ferruccio Selvaggio, shipping magnate extraordinaire, who, at thirty-two, is one of the richest men in the world. He's like a wrecking ball, rising so high so young, over the smashed remains of anyone who's dared stand in his way. Hence the nickname, which also happens to be the meaning of his aptly given names."

"That's according to you, of course." Luci smirked.

"That's according to common knowledge. He's a terror. But judging by our king's enthusiasm, it seems he's willing to overlook that fact—along with the other fact, that Ferruccio is a bastard, literally—if he'll only invest heavily enough in Castaldini."

"My, Stella, I hope nobody thinks you're the example of what royal blood does for a person," Luci said. "It would be so unfair if you gave us all a reputation for being stuck-up bitches."

Stella pouted. The perfect beauty was always putting on an act, oozing class and subtle sexuality, showing her true self only to other women, knowing men would think them jealous harpies if they criticized her. "Being a mongrel yourself, Luciana, you don't have to worry about that. But then, that makes you the perfect merchandise he's here to shop for. You have enough diluted blue blood that you might fit the bill in his bid to buy legitimacy. With what he has to offer in return, I say go for it."

As Luci continued to argue with Stella, Clarissa turned and walked away. Stella's vile words were like acid poured over the rawness of that incendiary moment. It didn't matter that it had all been in her mind. The damage was real.

She'd moved a good way through the crowd when something made her turn around.

He was heading toward where she'd been standing. Coming back for her? Had she been wrong about that second look? She began walking back.

Her feet gathered momentum as he zeroed in on Luciana and Stella. Would he ask them about her?

Then she was close enough to see the glazed look entering the women's eyes at being under his immediate influence, to hear the rumble of his deep voice, the predatory flirtation in it.

Something shriveled inside her, like a paper curling up as flames ate it to ashes. Her feet changed course again, quickened, until she was almost running as she exited the ballroom to the verandah. She breathed hard, snatching air into constricted lungs.

Stop it. You fool.

She'd imagined it all. The attraction *and* the antipathy. He'd been looking at Luciana all along. Or perhaps he looked at every woman the way she'd thought he'd looked at her.

Get ahold of yourself.

She slipped into the shadows, trying to do just that, to suppress tears she'd long thought had run dry.

She was a lousy excuse for a princess, but her father had asked her to take an active role in the court and in the kingdom, at his side, in her mother's place. It had been the first thing he'd asked of her in…ever. She was damned if she'd run out on him. Again.

She straightened her aching back, started to move—and walked into a wall of hot, hard muscle and maleness. *Him.*

She stumbled back, started to apologize, to sidestep him, air shearing into her lungs, chaos invading her synapses.

He blocked her escape route. He didn't touch her—he didn't need to. His very presence reached out and snared her in an inescapable embrace. And that was before her gaze streaked up to his, to find him looking down at her with that trance-inducing intensity.

The effect was the same as it had been during that first flash flood of recognition.

Her consciousness wavered. The world swirled around her as his eyes ate her up. Then his lips moved and she heard his voice, unobscured by the din of background chatter and music. Rich and fathomless, sweeping over her like a binding spell.

"I'm leaving. And you're not enjoying this reception any more than I am. Come with me."

She stared up at him. No one should be endowed with all

that. He was too…everything. He towered about ten inches above her five foot eight, his physique that of an Olympian, his face that of an avenging angel, planes and hollows and slashes of power and perfection, a being of bronze and gold and steel, who took her breath away and held it just out of reach.

Dangerous. And if he could do this to her with a look, he was beyond that. Lethal. But that wasn't just a look in his eyes. That was…unadulterated coveting. Pure possession.

It was what she'd imagined she'd seen before. But she hadn't imagined the cold way he'd looked at her afterward, or the way he'd gone straight to the other women who'd caught his eye.

What was he playing at? He must expect all women to lose their mental faculties at the sight of him, and fall to their knees at his approach. And after he'd conquered Luci and that scorpion Stella—who couldn't have been immune to him—he'd come after her. Why?

He took a tight step closer, practically vibrating with something vast and overwhelming. She could have sworn it was hunger, barely checked. And it would be unleashed at the slightest provocation—a gasp, a tremor.

She was incapable of any physical reaction, caught in stasis, waiting for his next words to reanimate her.

Suddenly, the spectacular wings of his eyebrows drew together. "You're uncertain whether you can trust me? Don't you know that you can?"

He was talking as if they knew each other. She would have found it the most natural thing in the world if this encounter had taken place immediately after that first glance. She had felt as if she'd known him, then.

When she remained staring up at him, mute, he exhaled. "I thought we didn't need formalities, that we could revel in this…" he made an eloquent gesture, from his heart to hers "…connection, without outside interference. Maybe I'm asking too much." He exhaled again. "Let's go inside. We'll find your father on the way out. He can vouch for me."

He knew who she was.

That was why he was out here rather than with the women who'd interested him for real. He wasn't here for her. He was here for Princess Clarissa D'Agostino, the king's daughter. Just like every other man who'd ever found out she was royalty.

Stella had said he wanted to add some blue-blooded legitimacy to his image. She might or might not be right. But Clarissa knew one thing. He didn't want *her.* And why should he?

Nobody had ever wanted her.

The hurt and humiliation finally forced an answer from her spastic lips. "That won't be necessary, *Signore* Selvaggio."

The heat and assurance in his gaze wavered. "You know me?"

"I know *of* you. Ferruccio Selvaggio, shipping magnate and potential investor in Castaldini."

His lips tugged, not into a smile, tension entering his gaze. "Right now I'm only the man who wants the pleasure of your company for the rest of the evening. Join me for dinner."

Not a request. A demand. One she would have stumbled over herself to accept if he hadn't bypassed her for her glamorous friend and relative, only to pursue her when he realized she better served whatever purpose he had in mind.

She tilted her face, as princesses were supposed to do to end unsavory situations, striving to project detached authority and nonnegotiable dismissal, for the first time managing to implement the teachings of two dozen etiquette instructors who'd begged to be relieved of the impossible duty of teaching her to act her part. "Thank you for the invitation, *Signore* Selvaggio. But my…situation doesn't allow me to…be with you. I'm sure you'll find someone else who can."

His whole body tensed and his nostrils flared as if he had braced himself against the force of a resounding slap. He understood. She wasn't talking about her situation tonight. She was giving him a taste of his own medicine. If he wanted her for who she was in society, she was letting him know she *didn't* want him for the same reason.

Heat seeped from his eyes, something almost scary flooding to fill the vacuum it left behind.

He finally shrugged. “Pity. But there may come a time when your…*situation* might not leave you any option but to…be with me.” With a nod of his awesome head, he pivoted, took a couple of relaxed steps away before he tossed a glance over his daunting shoulder. Then he murmured softly, menacingly, “Until then.”

One

The present

Finally.

The word reverberated in Ferruccio Selvaggio's head, spread in his blood along with the thick, bitter ooze of grim satisfaction.

He'd finally gotten Clarissa D'Agostino where he wanted her.

A supplicant coming to beg his favor. In—he flicked a glance at his Rolex—twenty minutes' time.

She couldn't be here soon enough. He'd been waiting too long for this moment. Six years. That was how long she'd evaded him. Snubbed him. The princess who thought his hard-won wealth and power not enough to raise him to the status of the men she deigned to mix with, men born with the right lineage. The blue blood who thought a bastard, no matter how rich and influential, not worthy of civility.

But despite all her haughty disdain, he had Princess High-and-Mighty coming to do his bidding. And if everything went according to plan—and he now possessed all the leverage to make sure it did—he'd have her doing his bidding far longer and in far more ways than she thought.

He'd have her, period.

He'd been fantasizing about having her ever since that first night he'd seen her. That first glance.

It had been his first time in the royal court. He'd been uncertain of his reception, of his reaction to being there. Most of the people there had been D'Agostinos. His so-called family.

But he didn't share their name. His parents hadn't had him the acceptable way, hadn't given the name to him. Others had given him the surname he used now. He'd been called by it so many times, it had stuck. So he'd made it legal.

The evidence that he was a D'Agostino had been presented to him long ago. At the time, he'd demanded public recognition. His parents had been willing to give him anything but that. He'd told them what to do with their love and offers of support. He'd survived so far without them. He'd make it on his own, make it to the top, the same way.

Finally he'd reached a height of success from which he thought it time to satisfy his curiosity. He wanted to see what it was like, the place that should have been his home. What they were like, the people who should have been his family. If he'd been missing anything. If he could make up for it if he had been; if he could grow the roots he'd never had.

He'd entered the king's court unannounced. By then, he'd had enough clout that he could walk in anywhere in the world and be welcomed. And the court had welcomed him. To this day, he remembered none of those who'd done so. Besides his meeting with the king, he remembered nothing before and nothing after he'd seen *her* across the teeming space.

She'd been wiping at something on the neckline of that ethereal violet dress. In profile, her face had been a study of concentration and consternation. He'd felt everything inside him prime, rev into awareness.

Stunned, not knowing what that upsurge meant, he'd needed to look her in the face, in the eyes. Then she'd turned, fulfilled his need. And something he'd always scoffed at had ripped through him. A bolt of attraction. More, of recognition. Of the one woman who translated his every fantasy into glorious reality.

Physically, she'd been the amalgam of all the endowments he'd never thought could be gathered in one being. Hair the color of Castaldini's beaches, streaked with rays of its sun, permeated by tones of the rich soil of its mountains. A body at once willowy and womanly, unconscious femininity screaming in its every line and curve. A face that embodied all his tastes and demands.

But it had been her eyes—which really had turned out to be violet, when he thought he'd imagined the color from that distance—and what he'd seen in them, that had snared him.

To think he'd thought they'd shown a reflection of his awareness, his discovery. He thought he'd seen more, too, a quality that had snapped the trap shut: Vulnerability.

Right. Clarissa D'Agostino was as vulnerable as an iceberg to the Titanic.

He still seethed to remember how he'd sought her, bared his need to have more of her, revealed his moronic belief in the existence of a connection between them that had transcended time and logic. He still burned at the memory of the moment he'd gotten what he deserved for such idiocy, when she'd stared at him as if he'd lost his mind, then told him to go find someone in a lesser...situation—who'd deem him good enough to...be with.

She'd told him that dozens of times since then. With every rejection of the invitations he'd never ceased to issue. Making them had become the masochistic lash he used every time he found his will to go on flagging, using the anger and frustration to keep on rising, keep on acquiring everything in his path. As he couldn't acquire her.

But now he finally would. One way or another.

He'd teach her a lesson. Many lessons. He'd take her down a few dozen pegs, and he'd revel in every one.

He braced his arms against the balustrade, cast his gaze into the distance. The sun's gold was starting to deepen as the star quickened its descent toward the endless expanse of liquid turquoise and emerald that was the southern Castaldinian Sea.

Another rush of bitter anticipation tumbled and sprayed through his system like the waves did on the shore. He wasn't here only for the spectacular vista the tower of his mansion afforded him. This was also the best vantage point from which to view the winding road over which she'd be brought to him….

Everything seemed to dim as the last three words replayed in his mind like a distorted old recording.

Brought to him. Not coming to him of her free will, unable to wait to see him, as she had in too many dreams to count.

What would he have felt if she'd been rushing here with hunger in her eyes, with longing on her lips?

If only…

His lips compressed as he tore his eyes away from the road and blindly roamed the view he could no longer see.

No. No *if onlys.* She'd made her choice that first night. Had reinforced it countless times throughout six interminable years.

Even if she changed her mind now, for whatever reason, it would be too late. Now only one thing mattered. That she had no choice. That there was no way she could reject him again. And he intended to savor every second of her downfall, starting—he snapped another look at his Rolex—ten minutes from now.

He pushed away from the balustrade, swung around.

Time to put the finishing touches to his plan.

"Until then."

The words, spoken like a pledge, a prophecy, in the lethal tone of a dangerous man, reverberated inside Clarissa's head.

They had done so for six years now.

Twenty-four hours ago, she'd found out that "then" had arrived.

Ferruccio Selvaggio had her cornered.

She exhaled and gazed through sunglasses and rioting hair

at the vista rushing by as the limo zoomed over the road that snaked parallel to the shore.

She knew the sun was turning flame orange and speeding on an intercept course with the sea, that the horizon would be changing into a thousand hues and the waters would be starting their transformation from aquamarine to royal blue.

She saw none of it. Her vision was turned inward, where there was nothing but gray chaos.

Calm down. Breathe.

She carefully drew in a stream of the fresh sea air that buffeted her face. Then again. And again.

And nothing. Taking one breath at a time wouldn't restore any measure of calm. It hadn't since yesterday. Since her father had made her cut short her first official mission to the States to give her the news. The shock of her life.

She thought she'd known the limit of her father's desperation to find himself a crown prince after his stroke. He'd proven her wrong.

The crown of Castaldini was by law not passed from father to son, but rather earned by merit. With the approval of the royal council, the current king would choose his successor from the royal D'Agonstino family—a man of impeccable reputation, sturdy health and no vices, solid lineage, a leader with character and charisma, and above all, a self-made success of the highest order.

She'd been the only one who hadn't been stunned when he'd announced his first candidate. Leandro, the prince whom eight years ago her father had declared renegade, stripped of his nationality and exiled. She'd thought Leandro the wisest choice of any candidate for the crown. It had been time to forget grievances and think of Castaldini's best interests. But when her father had wrestled the Council into making the offer, Leandro had done the unthinkable. He'd turned the power and responsibility down.

And her father had dropped another bomb. He had another

even more impossible candidate. Her oldest brother, Durante. And in an undreamed of precedent in Castaldinian history, he'd gotten the Council to amend the most fundamental part of the kingdom's constitution to make his son eligible for the crown.

She'd never been so excited. She'd always thought how unfairly absolute the laws of succession were, that while they protected Castaldini from unsuitable heirs, in Durante's case they were depriving it from having its best king ever. But the Council had voted, and the impossible had become possible.

Then Durante had come back with his bride-to-be, and Clarissa had even dared to hope that he and her father would work out their rift. Everything had looked like it would have a perfect happy ending for her family and for Castaldini.

Again the impossible had happened. They *had* sorted out their rift, but Durante had turned down the succession.

She'd tried to speak to him, but he hadn't been available for discussion as he'd prepared for his wedding and disappeared with his bride on an extended honeymoon. Clarissa had gone to the States, her father assuring her that he was working on securing the next candidate, the one he believed most suited to the job despite there being an even more insurmountable barrier to overcome to make the Council agree.

She hadn't been able to imagine who could possibly be better than Leandro or Durante. Then the king made her cut her mission short to drop the biggest bomb of all.

He'd gotten the Council to make an even more incredible amendment, allowing the king to extend another offer of the crown of Castaldini.

To Ferruccio Selvaggio.

She still didn't know how she hadn't collapsed in a heap of shock and confusion upon hearing that.

From what she'd heard in the media about Ferruccio, he was a man with no origins. All that was known about his parentage was that he'd been given up for adoption in Napoli when he was born.

But he'd never been adopted. By the time he was a difficult

six-year-old, he'd been placed in a foster home, the first of a dozen, until he ran away from the last one at age thirteen. He'd chosen to live the harshest of lives on the streets of Italian coastal cities and in Sicily and Sardinia rather than return to the system. Over the next two decades, he educated himself extensively and worked his way up to the highest echelons imaginable.

When his status had solidified, he'd come to Castaldini. Since then, he'd been a recurring figure in her father's court, and a constant one in her dreams and nightmares. Worse, his businesses in the kingdom now comprised almost one quarter of the national income.

When she'd told her father that that didn't make him king material, that Castaldini couldn't just waive the laws that had made it unique in the world for eight hundred years to have a king who only answered the financial criterion of the ancient laws of succession who wasn't a D'Agostino or even a Castaldinian, her father had dropped the biggest bomb yet.

Ferruccio *was* a D'Agostino.

The king had been entrusted with this fact before Ferruccio had first come to Castaldini. He'd told a select few, among them Durante and Paolo, her brothers; but knowing the delicate dynamics involved, he'd chosen not to divulge Ferruccio's parents' names so that the house he belonged to wouldn't suffer the repercussions of exhuming buried secrets.

After his stroke, he'd given the Council his word as proof of the fact. They'd argued that illegitimacy was by far the worst breach of the ancient laws that he'd asked them to commit in his quest to find the next king. They couldn't accept a bastard contender for the crown. But the king had made a solid case for Ferruccio otherwise.

Ferruccio was everything the king must be, he said, even more so than his first two choices. He was even more radically self-made, as his rise had been against what should have been insurmountable odds. He was a leader by nature, his shipping empire the largest in the world and his political powers far-reaching. At last the Council succumbed and made the offer.

Contrary to Durante and Leandro, Ferruccio had been instantly amenable to discussing that offer. But he'd refused to give a word of either consent or refusal. Before he would give either, he had terms to negotiate.

He would negotiate with only one Council member. Her.

Clarissa closed her eyes again on another eruption of fury.

How *dare* that arrogant jerk!

Castaldini was not only acknowledging him, it was offering him the incalculable honor and privilege of becoming its future king, and he had *terms?* What more did he want? A binding contract adding the island to his real estate acquisitions?

Not that that was too far-fetched. Among her shocking discoveries, she found out that he'd long ago purchased a huge chunk of Castaldinian soil. Three hundred square miles of the six thousand that made up the island. It didn't matter that this was the south eastern area that was said to be unreclaimable for being too mountainous, it was still five percent of the whole damn kingdom.

And why negotiate with her? She was the most junior Council member. Wasn't really even that, yet. She'd been made a member the day before she embarked on her trip to the States, a training mission that had been cut short, too.

But she knew why.

Now that Ferruccio was in a position of unprecedented power, he wanted to lord it over the D'Agostinos, the royal family, maybe over the whole nation he felt had spurned him. He wanted to lord it over her, too, the only female, she believed, who hadn't fallen flat on her face at his approach, quaked at his every glance, melted when he beckoned.

Well, she had... But *he* didn't know that. She hadn't let him know, and she thanked God for that daily. She hated to think what would have happened if she hadn't been forewarned of his true nature and intentions and had succumbed to the dictates of her desires that first time he'd expressed interest.

His ruthless reputation proclaimed him to be an overendowed, overprivileged, overeverything boor who believed people's—especially women's—only use was to throw themselves at his feet, follow his orders and satisfy his appetites before being discarded. He'd lost no sleep over her rejection, as evidenced by the constant stream of interchangeable hotties who'd been flitting in and out of his bed ever since.

Not that he'd taken no for answer. Her dismissal seemed to have roused the conqueror in him, and he'd continued to approach her despite her consistent refusals.

After she dared to decline his first invitation, she'd seen him everywhere she went during the week he spent on Castaldini. She hadn't been able to breathe until he left. Then he'd come back within a month to issue another invitation and had continued to do so whenever he returned, and even more when he hadn't. He kept asking her to hop over to Milan, Monaco or Madrid, to join him for a meal, Hong Kong or Tokyo or Rio De Janeiro to join him for the weekend, among a party or alone.

She turned him down every time, with one excuse or another, struggling to observe formal politeness and neutrality, since he was such an important man to her father and Castaldini.

But he'd left her that first night with the augury that there would come a time when she'd have no option but to do his bidding.

That time was finally here.

She wondered how he'd justified his demand to her father. He must have said something convincing, or her father wouldn't have been so matter-of-fact about it.

So he'd finally have his laugh. That had to be his objective. If there'd been a shadow of a doubt that he'd been pursuing her to freshen his image with a coat of legitimacy, it had evaporated. He was a D'Agostino, would be proclaimed the future king of Castaldini. There was no higher status or recognition he could aspire to.

The limo slowed down, and with it her streaking thoughts.

That only made her anger gain momentum again. She'd been fuming since he'd sent his aides to summon her. She'd grudgingly let them escort her to his jet. She hadn't found him onboard as she'd expected, had been stunned to find the jet taking off, whisking her away to his private part of the island without so much as an explanation or request for her token agreement.

And here she was. Approaching the only man-made construction and landscaping she'd seen in the last twenty minutes since the jet had landed at what was clearly a private airport.

There were no fences anywhere. The limo passed through a gate made by an opening in a row of towering cypress trees.

As they cruised down the driveway she realized the estate must cover hundreds of acres and the mansion at its middle must be over thirty thousand square feet. It sprawled in many levels, crouching over the highest point in the landscape, surrounded by manicured, mature gardens that on one side gave way to a mile-deep, golden beach, on another to the terrain where the road ended, and on the remaining sides to densely verdant groves ripe with fruit.

It felt like she was forging deeper into a tranquil paradise as they passed acres of oranges and tangerines, the fresh, tangy scent filling her.

The moment they stopped at the beginning of a stone path, she disembarked, more than usual unable to bear the pomp of ceremony.

Her chauffeur hurried to lead her on the path flanked by magnificent palms and a plethora of other Mediterranean flora to the entrance of the mansion. Her eyes wandered over its neo-Gothic stone facade as they neared. It looked as if it had been built centuries ago and transported through time the moment the last touch had been applied. The most characteristic features were the arched motif to all its windows, passageways and doors and the central tower.

She squinted up at the elaborate coat of arms that decorated the tower's top. She wondered what it was, if it had any significance, or if it was just something that had appealed to him. It did bear resemblance to the D'Agostino family's crest. Had he meant it that way, to express his affiliation, yet not wanted it to be the same, as he considered himself an outsider?

Her futile conjectures came to an end when the chauffeur opened the huge, arched antique oak door for her. She preceded him inside, but rather than following her, he closed the door behind her. She heard his steps receding quickly. Her lips tightened.

He'd delivered his master's package and ran away as if he were being pursued by some malevolent force. It seemed everyone who must populate this place, who took care of all the immaculateness she'd seen, had the same orders. She hadn't seen a soul so far.

She waited for Ferruccio to appear, her heart thudding. She'd never been totally alone with him. Even that first night when he'd followed her out to the seclusion of the verandah, masses of people had been within reach. She made sure he never found her alone from then on. Here in his domain where he ruled supreme, she felt cut off from the world. As she was sure he'd meant her to be. Another wave of resentment crashed over her.

And the worst part? She couldn't act on her antipathy. More than ever she had to observe the dictates of diplomacy. Her position on the Council demanded that she strip her demeanor of any personal reaction, save only what would serve her mission.

But with every second that he didn't appear, he was transforming that task from difficult to impossible.

Her hearing sharpened until every heartbeat was amplified to thunder in her ears. But she didn't hear approaching footsteps. There was only the distant drone of the waves and the tranquility of the internal courtyard in which she stood. It was at least two thousand square feet, paved in lava stones, lit with the impending sunset's red-gold beams, which filtered from arched and round windows inset in the walls just below its domed ceiling.

He wasn't coming. Not yet, at least. He must be letting her stew. She exhaled, moved. Might as well take a look around.

She strolled to the end of the courtyard, opened doors, her surprise rising as she found an olive press and wine-processing rooms. She wouldn't have thought he'd go to the trouble of making his own oil and wines.

Mulling over this discovery, she headed to the other side of the courtyard where a corridor of arched columns ended in five stone steps. These led down to an arrangement of expansive sitting rooms with a unique take on Roman décor, in a combination of stucco and stone walls, and strewn with luxurious couches and low tables.

She wondered if he entertained a lot, if one of his many unspecified-destination invitations had been to come join him here. She wondered how she would have reacted to this place if she'd come here ignorant of the truth of his intentions, breathless with anticipation, ready to be swept away by the spell of his domain, to sink into its sensory decadence.

Shaking her head at the pointlessness of her musings, at the stupidity of letting them depress her with what ifs, she crossed into an amazing dining room with a round bronze table and a circular stone platform for chairs, with pillow seating.

This section had a medieval feel, with wall torches and large white cushions abounding in every corner. The floors were layered in old Sicilian pottery tiles, the designs flowing into variations as she progressed through the rest of the ground floor. Huge stone fireplaces sprouted in strategic spots, though subtle evidence of state-of-the-art electric heating was also present.

But what really amazed her was some of the most ingeniously placed and painted trompe-l'oeil she'd ever seen in the walls and ceilings. The murals' optical illusions were almost indistinguishable from the three-dimensional imagery they depicted in depth and realism. They felt like portals into alternate realities.

She stopped in front of one, a tableau of a pigeon on a *fer forgé* windowsill, the glass behind it reflecting it and a distant sea and sky. It looked so real she almost thought the glass was there, did reflect that vista, that she could pet the gleaming feathers of the bird, that it would take flight if she tried.

Ferruccio must have spent untold millions here, from acquiring the land, to equipping it with a private airport and silk-smooth roads, to building that incredible edifice that must be maintained year-round so he'd find it in perfect condition whenever he hopped over, maybe a few days each season.

It was clear to her why he brought her here, and why he hadn't appeared yet. He was flaunting his wealth and power, giving her time for every detail to sink in, make its mark.

He'd picked the last woman on earth to be awed by affluence.

She lived in a palace, and she'd come to associate the grandeur that had surrounded her since birth with the anxiety and despair that had tainted her turbulent childhood. In fact, she'd been almost relieved that the opulence had long faded, with her father barely maintaining the parts of the palace that were national monuments. She sure wasn't about to swoon over pretentious extravagance.

But she grudgingly had to hand it to Ferruccio. This place wasn't pretentious. Or extravagant. It was a masterpiece of architecture and attention to detail but every article and line of design spoke of taste and discernment, everything so simple and unobtrusive it amalgamated into a retreat that promised enjoyment and ease to both mind and body.

Suddenly, ever fiber of her mind and body seemed to become a compass needle, obeying the magnetism that mushroomed at her back. She spun around.

And there he was. The man who'd ruled her every thought since the night she'd laid eyes on him, who'd manipulated her reactions and emotions with the slightest tug here, nudge there, just because he could.

He was standing at the mezzanine level gallery that overlooked the courtyard she'd wandered back to, looking down on her like a Roman deity would on a supplicant coming to beg his mercy.

She thought he'd stand there until she begged for real, for him to just come down and get this over with. Then, without a word, his eyes maintaining their lock on hers, he started moving toward the stone stairs. He descended soundlessly, effortlessly, his long legs turning the movement of taking each wide step into a performance of predatory grace.

Then he was striding toward her, his every step like an expanding shock wave, rattling her bones with reaction.

Was it possible that he had become more vigorous, more virile, that every time she saw him she'd find new things to marvel at, that his effect on her would keep intensifying? She'd thought him magnificent in the formal outfits she always saw him in. But in faded jeans and a partially unbuttoned denim shirt, he was…unfair.

She looked up at him, praying that her inner turmoil wouldn't be translated into an outward manifestation that he could read and exploit.

He stopped a breath away, took the rest of her breath away as his gaze sliced through her like a steel blade. Then his lips spread in the first smile he'd ever trained on her.

"*Principessa* Clarissa," he murmured, low and lethal, "It's such a delight to see your…situation has finally allowed you to…be with me."

Two

He remembered. What she'd said that first night.

Of *course* he did. And he was throwing it back in her face.

She bet the injury to his pride had been the prod that had kept him issuing those invitations, intent on breaking her resistance so that he could avenge what he must have considered a colossal insult—so that he'd keep his perfect score.

And he'd kept it. He'd made her bow to his will. She should have known he would. He'd gotten where he had by being inexorable.

She'd known that, yet thought there'd be no way he could prevail in this. She couldn't have imagined the developments that had led her here.

But even without them, she now believed he would have won eventually. Hadn't she studied his methods at length, both on her own and where they were taught in business school—to demonstrate the ultimate model of long-term, unrelenting, undetectable planning?

Even if she'd been dead wrong about her safety from his

octopoid reach, she'd been spot on about another thing: He *was* gloating. And there was not a thing she could do about it.

Not only that, but she had to be on her best behavior, answer with something unrelated, divert the dialogue away from personal hostilities. In short, she couldn't rise to his bait.

Then she opened her mouth. "What can I say? Life takes such…regrettable twists and turns. And downward spirals."

She almost groaned out loud. What was she *saying?* And in that long-suffering, condescending tone, too? He'd take it as provocation. And he'd be right. It was.

Sure enough, his lips tugged wider, the cool smile heating, the assessing, dispassionate eyes sparking. "Indeed. But I don't know about regrettable. I'm quite the fan of roller coasters."

She should keep her mouth shut, hope he'd take the conversation to safer areas. Even if he didn't and kept poking at her, she should nod and agree. Let him have his victory, let him rub her nose in it, shove its bitterness down her throat. She'd bet that was the "negotiations" he wanted to conduct—an extended session of having her here on his "terms," in a position where she couldn't say no or walk away. She should let him have his fill, get it over with.

Then she opened her mouth, and it seemed someone willful and inflammatory had hijacked her voice, which taunted in its husky tones, "You would be. It has taken a twisting, turning spiral upward with you. Apparently with no drop in sight."

His lips twitched as he pretended to suppress his mockery. "I should hope not. Can you imagine a fall from such heights?"

Dio, he was giving her more rope. She duly took it and secured it around her neck. Then she kicked the bucket. "Oh, how I can."

His mouth lost the fight with the sobriety he'd been forcing on it and spread wide, almost blinding her with a flash of white teeth and brutal charisma. "I see you've given it some serious thought. Seems you enjoyed the detailed visualization of such an event."

She gave up trying to rein in her responses, gave in, admitted her acrimony. "Enjoyment would be a mild term if such an event came to pass. It would be—how did you put it—such a delight."

She heard the fervent venom in her voice, knew he'd heard it, too. Everything stilled as he stared at her, probably unable to believe that anyone dared talk to him that way, princess or not.

Then suddenly, he threw his head back and guffawed.

It was her turn to stare, feeling as if one move now would snap the last tatters of tension holding her up.

She'd never seen him laugh. She hadn't known he was capable of such a human indulgence. She should have known he'd do it like he did everything else. Overridingly.

The sight and sound of his unbearably male amusement hit her between her eyes and forked a downward path through her heart and gut to lodge in her loins. The semiarousal that burned inside her just because he existed roared higher. Along with the blaze of her anger.

He was goading her into even more catastrophic antagonism, into giving him enough incriminating evidence to report back to her father and the Council that their newest addition was a disgrace to the body of power she represented and should be banned from public service forever.

And she didn't give a damn. Not anymore. He'd won. Six years of dangling himself before her, of pricking and prodding her periodically until she was inflamed and perpetually on the verge of an explosion, had taken their toll. She thought she'd been far from the breaking point. She was clearly way past it.

Ferruccio still chuckled, rich, dark reverberations from deep in his chest, annihilating what remained of her restraint. "Wouldn't your conscience prick you if you felt 'such a delight' in my downfall? Now that you know I'm a newfound family member?"

Clarissa rolled her eyes. "Don't remind me."

He hooted on another surge of amusement. "*Si. There* she is. I always knew that beneath all that impassive decorum you had the temper of a lioness. I kept wondering what could rile you enough to get you to unsheath your claws and slash away."

She harumphed, disgusted at her pathetic excuse for self-control, at his ability to peel it away. "Congratulations. You've succeeded in finding out. I hope you're enjoying your success."

"I've never enjoyed anything more. Ever."

"'Never' got the point across. Don't be redundant."

He laughed again. "What a cruel cousin you are."

"A *very* distant cousin."

His eyes seemed to turn to molten steel. "*Si.* In every way."

He was referring to her keeping him at an arm's to a continent's length all those years. As if he'd really cared.

"But you're not distant now, at least not in one sense." He took a step closer, his thigh almost touching her hip. She stumbled backward two steps. He lowered his gaze for a moment—as if debating closing the gap again—before raising his eyes. This time he almost did knock her off her feet. And that was before he added, deeply, smoothly, "See how easy it turned out to be?"

"What did? Being flown in to you like a package? One that you had dropped on your doorstep, to be left untended and unacknowledged until you stirred from your beauty sleep and puttered down to reluctantly receive it? Yeah, that sure didn't involve any effort on my part."

"You think there was any reluctance involved in my…receiving you? After I've gone to the trouble of insulting all the senior Council members by refusing to negotiate with anyone but you?"

"That's my proof that you welcomed my arrival? Try another one, Signore Selvaggio. The only insult you hurled was at me. The others must be thinking you asked for me because I'm the only Council member who's a young woman, the demographic where you reign supreme, and you think me the pushover who'll promise you rights to every Castaldinian citizen's immortal soul in return for your acceptance."

He snorted. "Now those are rights that might be worth my

while to investigate acquiring." Before she gave in to the urge to smack him, he added, "But if anyone thinks you a pushover, they need to be declared mentally incompetent. Whatever else you think of me, you know my mental faculties aren't among my dodgy areas."

She huffed. "Then they'll think something even worse. That you're exploiting the situation for a personal purpose, which must again have something to do with my being a woman, devaluating my position within the Council even more."

As the word "position" left her mouth, his gaze traveled down her body. Her throat closed at what she saw there, in her own mind's eye. His gaze finally burned a path back up to her eyes, the hewn planes of his face simmering as they had that first night. When she thought she'd imagined it. She wasn't imagining it now.

"Your...*position* is quite safe, I assure you. You should know by now that no matter what the textbooks they stuffed your mind with in business school said, in the real world, the personal factor is what ends up making or breaking business deals. If the Council thinks I'm being personal about you being a woman, they'll think it only natural, even logical. After all, what kind of a businessman would I be if I didn't maximize on my opportunities? If I didn't use my stones to hit as many birds as possible?"

"I should have known you wouldn't even bother to deny it."

He gave her an enigmatic look. "I'm not admitting it, either. So it's all open to interpretation. And here's a third one: That I asked for you because I want to talk to someone close to my own age, rather than with men my absentee father's age or older."

Her chest suddenly felt as if it had caved in. It was that distress again, the one thing that had always stopped her from despising him completely. The knowledge that he'd grown up without a father, or any parents at all.

How many times had she imagined him as a young boy desperately in need of the firm and loving guidance and protection of a father figure, and knowing he'd never have that? How many times had she woken up with tears in her eyes imagining the fear and loneliness he must have suffered until he'd grown that impenetrable shell of capability and ruthlessness that had seen him through his meteoric rise? How hard had she struggled to separate her empathy with the tormented child he'd been from her antipathy toward the man he'd become?

When she made no answer, his lips twisted. "Here's a fourth one. That you're the easiest Council member on my eyes…on all my senses."

She was glad to hook onto something to drag her out of her turmoil. "Now *that* I can buy. Considering the alternatives."

His eyebrows rose in astonishment. She could swear it was genuine. "You think the I'd only pick you when the alternatives are sour-faced older men and their feminine counterparts?"

She bit her tongue to stop herself from blurting out that she didn't think it, she *knew* it. Hadn't he just said what amounted to that? Even if he hadn't, she knew that when there'd been more glamorous options, she hadn't featured as one at all. She'd made sure of that.

Pathetic wretch that she was, she'd sought Luci's version of what had happened that night, hoping she'd misinterpreted what she'd witnessed. Luci had only confirmed her worst suspicions.

Ferruccio had come on hot and heavy, expressed interest in both Luci and Stella. At the same time. Luci had said he'd been so overpowering that she'd found herself wondering whether she *could* share a man, and with the dreaded Stella, of all women, too. She'd said she thought Stella herself had been tempted. That was, for the fleeting moments before he suddenly moved on without a look back.

Throughout the years, Clarissa had seen him acting as if he'd never said a word in private to either woman, let alone propositioned them so outrageously. That had reaffirmed her belief that he went through life making sure all women were his for the taking, but not actually taking up with anyone whose connections might cause him trouble. *Her* only lure had been that she was the king's daughter, and later on that she was the only woman who'd told him no. And if she thought she'd seen something in his eyes every time he caught her gaze—something that told her what he'd do with her if he ever got her alone—she reminded herself of the facts, concluded that she'd been superimposing her fantasies on his expression. As she must be now.

"No more contentiousness, *Principessa?* Hmm, I think I know why." His gaze dropped to her lips, clung, until she felt his mouth was there, drawing hard on her flesh until it swelled, ached, until *she* ached for him to do it for real. "You're… hungry."

Alarm erupted, followed by a flood of mortification. He knew. Or was he guessing, based on universal female response to him?

Before she could say anything, he took her elbow in a phantom grip. "Come. Let me feed you, get you back in fighting form."

Food. He'd meant hungry for *food.*

She was so relieved she let him guide her without a word.

She lost all sense of direction as he led her through his mansion, until they reached another huge oak door. She followed him through it, her every movement feeling controlled by his will.

Minutes later, they came to an elevated, open-air deck overlooking a stunning, symmetrical landscaped scene. Its centerpiece was a gigantic rectangular pool with a semicircular protrusion at its near end, glittering pure aquamarine in the declining sun. Its lava stone and mosaic periphery segued at its far end into a cleared passage between olive groves that continued until it melted into the vegetation-covered mountain in the distance. To the left, the groves gave way to dunes of pure gold, leading down to the serpentine shore and the azure and emerald waters.

She stopped, paralyzed by the magnificence of the sight.

She'd been raised on this island, but she never knew it still had such pristine natural places. The contrast with such lavish human design was breathtaking. But it was the seclusion that intensified that otherworldly feel. She'd never been anywhere so totally devoid of people. It felt as if they were the only man and woman on Earth.

The side of her face felt as if it were burning. She tore her eyes away from the scene, blinked up at him. She found him brooding down at her, his eyes heavy with so much emotion she didn't understand. Didn't want to understand.

He reached out a hand as if he was going to cup her cheek. At the last moment, he swept a lock of her long hair from her flaming face, tucked it with extreme care behind her ear. "You like?"

She swallowed, her heart spiraling in a nosedive like a shot-down plane. "I'm alive, am I not? I have to like."

His lips twitched. His eyes didn't change expression, seemed bent on liquefying her. Then he reached for her hand.

She felt as if he'd electrocuted her as he strode ahead, had her almost running behind him. She gurgled something about his legs being longer than hers. He turned as he slowed down, his smile riddling her vision in spots of blindness.

He had them circumventing the pool before taking one of the passageways that ran parallel to the groves and ended up at the edge of the beach. He suddenly stopped.

She rocked on her heels as he dropped to his haunches. Before she could process his action, he took her hands, placed them on his shoulders. She gaped as he lifted her right foot off the ground. Breath deserted her as he so slowly, so gently slid off her high-heeled sandal strap. The sandal fell off her suddenly stinging foot into his hand. Her toes curled, a gasp tearing from her. He looked up, noted her distress. Then he closed his hand over her foot, raised it, his lips parting, filling with sensuality.

He was going to…to… She couldn't let him or she'd…she'd…

She lost her balance, forced him to let her regain her footing. She leaned heavily on his shoulders so she wouldn't keel over him, electricity roaring from where her fingertips clutched their daunting power to zap incapacitation throughout her nervous system. He pressed her hands harder to his shoulders before repeating the de-sandaling ritual on her other foot.

When she was sure she would faint, he let her foot down, rose, bent and took his own sneakers off, placed them at the sand's edge with her sandals and spread his arm, inviting her to walk on.

She stumbled forward a few steps before she gasped, stopped.

The feeling of the powdered gold beneath her feet, its warmth and complex texture, its gritty softness, its resilient malleability heightened her sensory tumult.

He turned her toward him, his gaze solicitous. "Did you step on something? Are you hurt?"

Before she could answer he swooped down again, inspected one foot then the other, feeling for injuries or foreign bodies.

An uproar swept through her at his action, at the sight of his eyebrows drawn and his head bent in such concentration, the severely trimmed raven luxury of his mane gleaming copper in the sun as his perfectly formed fingers traced over her soles.

She was about to cry out that she was fine, when he heaved up to his feet, and in the same movement swept her up in his arms.

She went limp with shock.

He'd never touched her before. She hadn't even let him shake her hand. She thought she knew how dangerous it would be to have any physical contact with him. She'd known nothing. Feeling his flesh pressed on hers, his heat and scent invading her senses…it was too much.

She choked out, "Put me down—I'm OK."

He frowned. "Then why did you jerk to a stop like that? Why did you look so…distressed?"

"I was just…surprised. I—I've never felt anything like this."

His eyes narrowed. "You've never felt sand beneath your feet?"

She gulped, shook her head. "I…no."

"You've lived most of your life on a Mediterranean island

legendary for its sea and shores. How is it possible you never ran barefoot on the beach? Never swam in the sea?"

"I...uh...just didn't. The sea hasn't been part of my life."

"How was it even avoidable? Going to the beach is part of most people's childhoods, especially in seaside countries."

Her discomfort rose with every word. She wanted this conversation, and what it made her think of, what it could reveal, to be over. "I'm not 'most people.'"

"You mean because you're royal? That doesn't make sense. Durante and Paolo have both told me they spent much of their childhoods soaking in the sea and baking in the sun. And on Castaldini, royals aren't pursued and encroached on as they are in other countries. Even if you had been, your father could have provided a private beach for your use."

"I—I sunburn easily. I spent most of my childhood inside the palace. I'm almost always indoors, even now."

His gaze sluiced over her like silky, warm water, lingering on each inch of visible skin, making her want to moan with the pleasure of his visual caress. "Your skin is the finest and softest that I've ever seen. Or touched." His lids grew heavier as he smoothed the expanse of skin where her jacket and the form-fitting top beneath it had ridden up at her back. She stiffened with the blow of sensation. He gathered her more securely to him. "But it isn't the type prone to sunburning. In fact, I think you'd tan spectacularly."

His compliment went straight to her every hunger and vulnerability. Confusion over his motivation gave way to intense pleasure and self-consciousness. "I probably got badly burned once, when I was too young to remember. That and an over-protective mother kept me indoors from then on."

He gave her a long look, eloquent with disbelief. Out loud he said, "And you just agreed? You didn't want to rebel, seek all the freedoms and pleasures the sea has to offer? Doesn't sound like the Clarissa D'Agostino I know."

"Uh...you have a very rosy picture of the life of a princess."

"You mean I can't appreciate the impositions you had, and still have to put up with, as part and parcel of your status?" She braced herself for the frustration his next words would provoke. Everyone, especially men, had always said they understood how it had been for her, had tried to…console her for being such a poor, oppressed royal girl. His next words sent her preconceptions scattering. "No, I can't. I can only imagine some of them. But, since I never thought running on the beach and swimming in the sea were among the things you had to forgo, I must have imagined quite wrong. Even if I didn't, only you can speak of your experience."

She blinked back hot tears. He *had* understood. Something she'd never thought she'd ever feel toward him spread its balmy coolness inside her chest: thankfulness.

She bit her lip, nodded. "Whatever the reason, I never developed any fascination for the sea."

"You're fascinated now."

She tore her gaze away from his all-knowing one, cast it wide.

He was right. She'd never felt this thrill at witnessing what had always been there since she'd been born. She felt she was experiencing it all with new senses. With a few word of soul-searing insight, he'd made her realize the deprivation she'd suffered, of something so rich with pleasures, so available to anyone. Just being so close to him, his hands hugging her behind her knees and back, her palm still resting over his heart feeling it pumping steadily, as if he hadn't covered half a mile of beach with her in his arms, had made her… *Dio,* she was still in his arms!

She couldn't take one more second of this. She began to wriggle to free herself and he suddenly stopped, whispered, "Watch."

She jerked toward the point his eyes were fixed on. They were at the top of a dune where the shore extended to her vision's limit. She held her breath, felt him holding his as the red sun seemed to accelerate toward the darkening azure waters.

Then they touched, seemed to melt into one another, and he exhaled, molded her closer, as if to echo the celestial embrace.

A long moment passed as they shared the evocative display of sheer beauty, before she at last insisted he put her down.

He tightened his hold. "You're sure you're not uncomfortable walking barefoot on the sand?"

"It really was just a shock how good it felt."

A strange watchfulness descended on his face. Then he slowly released her, his eyes clinging to her face as if he wanted to record her reaction, memorize every nuance passing through her.

For the first time, she didn't want to hide her responses from him. She felt he had a right to witness them, in return for this gift he'd given her.

She moaned in pleasure as she again felt the sand flow between her toes, tickling her skin and massaging her soles.

The feeling was incredible, energizing. She gave in to it, to the unadulterated freedom and vitality it imbued her with.

She whooped, giggled, ran.

With every bound on the magical medium she'd lived her life looking at and never seeing, never experiencing, a burst of speed poured into her limbs. She heard his deep chuckles pursuing her. Unfettered laughter escaped her in response. And if a voice told her she must have plummeted into a parallel universe, to be running on a beach with Ferruccio Selvaggio chasing after her, it was silenced as soon as it spoke up. So what, if it felt this good?

Then she cleared another dune and saw it by the gently frothing waves. A huge circle of torch-topped, polished brass poles with a table set for two in its middle.

She turned to him in excitement, then sped ahead, the setup's details coming into focus. A lavender silk tablecloth draped the table, undulated like something alive in the gentle breeze. Gleaming black plates contrasted with its dreamy hue, while glittering silver utensils and crystal glasses added flashes of splendor. A buffet was set to the side.

She arrived at the table, swung around and grinned at him as he caught up with her, her breathing and heartbeat accelerating under the effect of his approach rather than from exertion.

His breathing was a bit quicker, but even, easy, his eyes gleaming silver with exhilaration. "Not only do you run like a lioness in that constrictive skirt, but you beat me, too. How fast would you be in something suitable?"

More heat rushed to her head, her cheeks. "It isn't that constrictive. And you weren't trying to outrun me."

He huffed a chuckle. "I gave it a good shot, believe me. I'm pretty fast. But you're much faster."

Her grin widened with pleasure at the ease with which he admitted she'd beaten him, his obvious enjoyment of the fact even. "I'll tell you my secret so you won't feel bad about it. I held my university's record in the indoor pentathlon for three consecutive years, and the regional one for two of those."

He looked genuinely impressed. Even though she got the feeling he already knew that. "And it's clear you've kept in shape ever since." His eyes again detailed how much said "shape" pleased them. "And now you'll add outdoor events to your repertoire. Including swimming in the sea. With me." She opened her mouth, closed it, the images his words had playing in her mind's eye turning her mute. Suddenly his smile's wattage spiked. "I bet you've crossed from hungry to starving after the unexpected exercise."

He tugged her to the buffet, exposed hot and cold serving plates, piled her plate with mouthwatering delicacies. She didn't protest. After going without more than a cup of tea since seeing her father yesterday, she *was* famished.

What followed was something she'd only dreamed of.

Even in fantasy, it had never been so easy, so natural. So unbelievable. They ate and exchanged anecdotes about their lives, opinions about almost everything, agreed, teased, laughed, and she found herself with the man she'd seen that first time—the one she'd felt connected to. Before everything had crashed around her ears and remained there in ruins for the past six years.

Now it was as if the years hadn't passed in tension and avoidance, as if this was the natural progression of that moment she'd thought so enchanted. And it did feel enchanted, yet more real than anything she'd ever experienced. *He* felt real. His real self, not the persona he projected when he moved through the ultra-formal settings where she'd made sure they always met with the buffer of her family around. Now that he was away from it all, he showed her sides of him she hadn't suspected existed, every glimpse enthralling her, embroiling her in the exhilaration of tangling with his wickedness and wit.

Sunset had morphed into the most breathtaking twilight she'd ever witnessed. The impossibly clear, totally unpolluted skies became a sweeping canvas of hues jeweled by strokes and patterns of clouds that had seemed to materialize just to reflect and prism the lingering light into ephemeral paintings that stunned the senses. Then it all gradually faded under the dominion of darkness until moonless, star-blazing night had taken over. She was dazzled by the spell of the ambiance, but more so by her companion.

He'd just served her fresh watermelon, grown on the land everyone had given up as irreclaimable, among many vital crops of which she'd seen oranges, tangerines, olives and grapes. As he sat down she commented on that before resuming her comments on one of his latest takeovers, and he leaned back in his chair, grinning.

"I always let my opponents fight me until they're exhausted, all the while showing them how sweet surrender would be. Then, when I judge they've had enough, I move in, and at that point they're ecstatic for me to take over."

Air escaped her lungs in a rush. She couldn't draw it back.

That could describe what he'd been doing to her.

It could, because it did.

Dio, what a fool she was. She should have known, when it

had all felt too good to be true, when he'd started lavishing praise and understanding on her.

He had done so to make her putty in his hands. And he'd succeeded. He'd made her forget what he was, the danger he posed to her, the reason she was here. He hadn't just overcome her antipathy and turned its tide into acceptance and eagerness, he'd negated reason and memory, silenced every caution. And he'd done it imperceptibly.

She had to surface from under his spell, run for her emotional and psychological survival. She had to get back on track, do what she'd come here to do. Quit playing the game by his rules, according to his agenda. Whatever that was.

Disillusionment became venom as it exited her lips. "That's interesting, how you get your conquests to become your willing thralls. Thanks for sharing that insider tidbit. Especially as it gives me the opening to get to the point of this...charming evening. Now that we've gotten the dinner you've been harping on for years out of the way, I hope you're satisfied and we can finally get down to discussing something important." His eyes drained of the warmth that had ignited them for the past hours. She braced against the moronic urge to soften her tone, to see his eyes fill with that fake intimacy again. "So...go ahead. Negotiate. I can't wait to hear your 'terms'. They should be...entertaining."

Ferruccio almost flinched. He felt as if she'd kicked him in the gut. And she had. Figuratively speaking.

After the first shock passed, rage crashed over him.

How had this happened? He'd set out to lull her, to overcome her resistance. Where had it all taken such a sharp detour, so that he'd been the one who'd been lulled, who hadn't seen this coming?

For the past hours he'd forgotten his harsh intentions. He'd gradually drowned in the pleasure of her nearness as she'd shown him a persona that combined the vulnerability he'd thought he'd seen that first night with a steel shield of will and wit, wrapped around a core of fun and warmth and passion.

And it had just been another of her masks.

How had she blindsided him again? He could still swear she'd finally taken off all her masks and shown him her true self. Which her own words now told him was premium self-delusion.

She'd taunted him with the memory of his rejected invitations, intimating she'd considered them the undignified and *unimportant* pursuit of an unacceptable suitor, and that this evening was her way of giving him what he'd been "harping" on, to humor him, because of the situation she'd been forced into. And would he now stop behaving irrationally?

Her sarcasm sent the beast inside him clawing out of his gut. Disappointment spilled from there to burn his insides.

She hadn't been enjoying herself, had been leading him on to equalize the balance of power so that she wouldn't be the beggar here. She was trying to set a record that, no matter what upper hand he held now, between them, he'd get nothing but the condescension he deserved. It was clear it didn't matter that he was a D'Agostino. He remained a bastard in her eyes.

She really had no idea who she was dealing with, how out of her depth she was. He might be cultured and suave on the surface, but he was a street fighter at heart. Playing against odds she couldn't begin to imagine in her wildest nightmares, to win at any cost was what he did. And it was time to do so.

It was time to make her regret her snobbery.

His bared his teeth in a smile he knew would chill her bones as it had so many, from politicians to tycoons to mafia dons. "You want to negotiate, *Principessa?* By all means. And since you're so enthusiastic to hear my terms, here they are. Or here *it* is. I have one term for taking the succession. That I take you with it."

Three

"You're insane."

Ferruccio leaned back in his chair, stuck his hands in his pockets and indolently surveyed Clarissa, savoring her shock and indignation as she choked on his declaration.

"Am I, now? Hmm. Literally all the financial world disagrees with your verdict."

"That's because you're so intelligent that you manage to hide your insanity. And it's possible to be a financial genius and a raving lunatic all at once."

He feigned boredom even as he cursed himself for letting her barbs prick him. "Maybe. But you've heard my term, Clarissa. And it should answer all your questions about why I asked for you, why I summoned you here. To pay you the courtesy of demanding it directly from you, rather than from your father and his Council."

Her mouth opened on a silent O. The lust that had been eating through him like slow acid all those years poured through his system in seething torrents. Imaginings of what devouring those dimpled lips would be like had ratcheted to a new dimension after watching them do so many things he'd never seen them do before—thin, curl, purse, tremble, quirk, spread in smiles and laughter, get bitten by those pearls she had for teeth, licked by that tantalizing-in-every-way tongue….

As for that vital body of hers, which had grown progressively more voluptuous as he'd burned for her from afar, he now knew how limited his fantasies of possessing it had been. Now that it had filled his arms, pressed against his flesh, trembled in his hold, buzzed with what he knew, against all her condescension and disdain, had been as unbridled a hunger as his own, he knew. Possessing it would be beyond anything he'd experienced or dreamed about.

Which meant one thing. Pulverizing her resistance had just turned from a resolution to a necessity.

At last, she seethed, "You think they would have even considered your crazy demand? What do you think this is, the Middle Ages?"

He reached out and calmly poured himself a glass of pomegranate juice, quirked an eyebrow at her over the rim after the first sip. "This juice shares so much with you. The richness of the complex flavors that make it up, the sour sweetness."

Her hands fisted on the table. "Spare me the false praise."

"I won't spare you anything." He watched his multifaceted threat invade her sculpted cheeks with a peach hue that burned bright, even in the dimness of the flickering firelight, made him struggle not to storm up and go devour it and her. "You really think I'd make such a demand if I had any doubt I'd obtain it? You claim to have studied my methods, Clarissa. Didn't your extensive studies and all those postgraduate degrees reveal that I don't make a move if I'm not one hundred percent certain of its success?"

She sank her teeth into her lower lip to control the tremor that took hold of it. His own twitched with a surge of intoxication. What could he say? It was such a delight to see her with her composure shattered, with anger, dread and arousal tearing at her.

Just as he thought she'd realized she was outclassed and overpowered, those uncanny eyes seemed to pulse purple with each flare of the flames. "My studies and degrees also revealed another thing, Signore Selvaggio. That sooner or later, even impervious, unstoppable business gods miscalculate. As you did this time. Big time. I'm not some commodity Castaldini can bestow on you as a side benefit. And I sure as hell am not volunteering myself as an incentive to sweeten the deal."

So. She wasn't cowed yet. *Bene.* In fact, it was great that she wasn't. He would have been seriously disappointed if he'd won that easily. He hated easy victory. And when it came to her, after all the years of frustration she'd put him through, he wanted—no, *needed*—her surrender to be a struggle. That way, the pleasure of her capitulation, when it came, would be all the more intense.

He was going to revel in this. Big time, like she'd said.

Time to play hardball.

The exhilaration of taking the skirmish to the next level danced on his lips. "Let me share a fact of life, *Principessa.* One from real life, not the sterilized, rarefied version it seems you've lived for all of yours. I don't need the crown. It's the crown that needs me. Desperately. That's why you're here. That's why you have no option but to abide by my terms and demands, to do everything I tell you to." He knew he had that serene look on his face that lions had on theirs as they took down their kill. He savored stressing his point. "Everything."

Clarissa's heart stopped for what must be the hundredth time today.

After a couple of dropped beats, it burst into another stumbling gallop that pushed no blood to her head, that left her feeling she was teetering on the verge of oblivion.

This wasn't happening. This *couldn't* be happening. He couldn't have said all he'd said. This *was* insane.

And he was watching her with the same coldness with which

he'd once looked at her across the ballroom on that first night. Which made it all crazier. Why was he even demanding this, her, if that was what he really felt toward her?

She struggled to keep hysteria from tingeing her voice and features. "I said that should be entertaining. And it is. You think you're irreplaceable, don't you? Well, you're not. My father is just going through his list of candidates. In case you didn't know already, you—in spite of your belief in your own indispensability—didn't rank first there. You merely happened to be third."

He took another sip of his juice, savored it slowly, made her imagine what he no doubt meant her to, those lips on her every secret, savoring *her,* before he murmured languidly, "Third *and* last."

"You really have an inflated sense of your own importance, don't you? Figures. Too many billions can do that to a man."

"When they're not inherited, and have been gained through legal venues, it's safe to say they do indicate indisputable personal value."

"Legal? Are you absolutely certain about that?" The look he gave her sent shivers of alarm, almost fear, zigzagging through her. She'd crossed a line.

She didn't give an ant's leg. Just as he didn't, about her or how she felt. "May you live happily ever after with your indisputable personal value, Signore Selvaggio. We'll find someone else. Someone who won't play cheap games when he's offered something as incalculable as the honor and privilege of the crown of Castaldini."

The danger in his eyes switched off, but the benevolence in the smile he bestowed on her was far worse. She felt her blood freezing in her arteries. "Good luck with that."

She stilled, the ice spreading. "What do you mean? And quit being cryptic. If you have something to say, then say it."

He gave a lazy shrug. "I don't have anything more to say. You know the rest, even though you're pretending not to. Contrary to what you accused me of, and unlike you, I don't play games."

"What are you *talking* about? What's that 'rest' I'm supposed to know?" she snapped.

His gaze sharpened, the steel luminosity of his irises flaring and subsiding with the flames of the torches until it seemed that the shifting shadows and golden lights they cast over his face would expose some supernatural entity that his magnificent body housed—one who examined her with brooding, malignant amusement.

Suddenly he threw his head back and laughed—a harsh, ugly sound so unlike his laughter during the past hours. Despite everything, this confirmation of the loss of the illusion of harmony and affinity they'd shared sent regret skewering through her.

"*Dio santo, sei serio.* You're serious. You know nothing. They left you in the dark, the old jackals. That explains everything. Why you think you can be your usual scathing self with me. They didn't warn that you they can't afford for you to alienate their last option. How remiss of them."

"That isn't true. It can't be. Someone else w—"

He cut her trembling protest short "—would bring about the end of Castaldini as we know it. No other man of Castaldinian origins or with the prerequisite D'Agostino blood—whether obtained on the right side of the sheets or not—possesses enough power to drive away the kingdom's external enemies and to defuse the internal conflicts. But I have my own empire, to which I owe my allegiance. On the other hand, even you can work out that I don't owe Castaldini or its people any measure of that. So don't play the honor and privilege card with me. I'm not in any way duty or honor bound to take on the responsibility of safeguarding Castaldini's crown and future. If I'm to accept doing your kingdom that 'incalculable' favor, I demand an 'incentive to sweeten the deal,' as you put it. And you're it."

She stared at him, at the face of his serene cruelty, his

absolute certainty, the tremors she'd been struggling to hold back breaking free, starting to rattle her bones.

He went on as if he was auguring something as trivial as a soccer game's outcome. "If you refuse, you can go back to your precious father and Council with my refusal, and let them pick someone else from the inadequate choices they've already rejected for the best of reasons, and let Castaldini go to hell."

He couldn't be lying about all this, could he? But maybe he didn't consider it lying, just maneuvering her by any means necessary to corner her. He was a master manipulator, after all.

And he wasn't even finished. He went on, and she discovered he'd saved the worst for last. "And when Castaldini is in ruins, maybe becomes some second-rate, exploited annex to one of the surrounding nations panting to drain its riches into their resource-poor, overpopulated, debt-ridden bellies, I'll still come after you. And I will have you. The crown will be lost, but you'll be mine in the end, Clarissa."

She was panting by the time he finished. Quaking. Then it all blurted out of her, all the indignation and distress he'd so expertly inflamed beyond the danger zone. "You're the one who can get lost, or can go to hell, Ferruccio Selvaggio—or D'Agostino, or whatever your name is. Be sure to take your toxic conceit and cruelty with you. Castaldini will survive without your oh-so-vital intervention, and you're not coming near me…."

Her tirade choked off into panting silence. It wasn't because he'd made any threatening move. It was his very tranquility, as he leaned forward, placed his glass on the table then heaved up to his feet, that made her every cell scream with alarm. Each movement was the measured advance of a predator with all the time in the world to pounce on his prey. Then he did.

He stopped by her, leaned down, took her hand and pulled her out of her chair and onto her feet.

"Wh-what are you doing?" she sputtered.

"What I should have done years ago."

He gave her a firm tug, slammed her against his body. Before she could draw another breath, one of his hands slipped into the hair at her nape, twisted there, immobilizing her head, tilting her face upward, the other trailing a heavy path of possession down to her buttocks. Then, as he held her prisoner, exerting no force but that of his will, he let her see it—the beast he kept hidden under the civilized veneer, its cunning savagery having assured his survival in hell, conquering of it, before being unleashed on this realm. The beast was hungry—and she was the meal it craved.

Holding her stunned gaze, his own crackling with the first unchecked emotions he'd let her see there, he lowered his head.

She felt as if she were in the path of a comet, that she'd disintegrate at impact. At the last moment before his lips took hers, she averted her face in an act of pure survival.

His lips landed on her cheek, at the corner of her mouth, with a chain reaction of insistent, escalating voracity. The feel of his lips on her flesh, the gust of his breath filling her with his scent and virility, left her suffering a widespread synaptic disruption. It was as bad as being a few feet from ground zero. Then he took his destruction to another level.

The hand on her lower back pressed her into him. Before she could deal with the blow of sensations at feeling his arousal against her belly, he relinquished his hold on her head, combed his fingers through her hair, over and over, sending pleasure cascading from every hair root, before that hand caressed her back, on its way to delving beneath her jacket and top.

She moaned a sound she'd never before produced, as the hard heat of his fingers splayed against her back, a part of her she'd never thought sensitive. Every inch of skin he imprinted felt moments away from the spontaneous generation of fire. She jerked away to escape, then pressed back for more. And he took his onslaught to the next level.

His other hand yanked up her skirt, cupped her buttocks through her panties and hauled her up against him. She gasped as she experienced weightlessness for the first time, then gasped louder as he ground the steel of his erection against her melting core. Something scalding rumbled from his depths as he tugged at one thigh, opened her around his hips for better access, splaying her for his thrusts. The hand at her back plastered her heaving chest against his, then he started rubbing against her. Her breasts swelled until they felt they'd burst, until the abrasion of her clothes, his shirt and the power it housed turned her nipples into pinpoints of agony.

She writhed in his hold, whimpered as he ravaged her neck in suckles that would leave their mark, that sent pleasure hurtling through her blood with each savage pull.

All existence converged on him, became him, his body and breath, his hands and mouth, as he tested her flesh and responses, tasted them, took over her will. She was no longer herself, but a mass of needs wrapped around him, open to him, his to exploit and plunder. There was nothing more to hear but his voracious growls and her distressed moans, their thundering blood and strident breathing as he raised her and slid her down his body in leisurely excursions, had her riding his erection through their clothing. Her top had somehow been peeled up and he dipped his head and took her nipples, one after the other, through her bra in massaging nips, sending ecstasy corkscrewing through her.

Her fingers buzzed as if they'd turned to live wires, and only digging them into his flesh could ground the excess charge. Her moans became a drone interrupted by sharp intakes of breath. The flowing throb between her legs escalated into pounding, needing something, anything, *everything,* to assuage it. When it tipped from discomfort into pain, she cried out his name, begged, she didn't know for what. He shuddered beneath her as he snapped his head up, crashed his lips on her wide-open mouth in a hot, moist vice, and thrust deep.

She plunged into his taste, rode rapids of delight as his tongue invaded her, taught hers to rub and duel and drink deeper of the fount of endless sensation, as his lips and teeth mastered her, gave her and took her and finished her.

This was nothing like the slow seduction she'd fantasized about. This was an invasion, a ravaging, and it catapulted her into a frenzy of need, an inferno of hunger. She wanted… wanted him to never stop, to do anything and everything to her, to take more, all.

She'd dreaded him and dreamed of him for too damned long. In her dreams, he'd always told her how much he wanted her, couldn't wait for her, but still lavished care and tenderness on her, in the only way she'd thought she could feel pleasure. Now he'd given her this. Overwhelming, no preliminaries, no boundaries, just raw need, unbridled ecstasy. Light years better, hotter than what she'd tormented herself with all these years, the insipid fantasies she'd thought the height of eroticism. She should have known he'd pulverize her expectations, as he took her and soared far beyond anything she could have imagined.

And if not for the debate that had finally pushed him to override her resistance, to no longer give her a choice…

Something cold and ugly seeped through her delirium. A memory. A realization. How this had started. As a measure to end that debate.

He'd gauged perfectly, as he always did, that this was the way to decimate her resistance, to take her over, mind and body.

And he'd been right. She'd succumbed to the hunger she'd been struggling against during all those years she spent escaping him.

He'd made her forget again why she had, how angry she'd been. At him, for pulling her strings when he didn't see her as a human being, just an asset, and at herself for knowing that and *still* yearning for him.

But her resistance was about far more than refusing to be another notch on his mile-long bedpost. It wasn't about pride. It was about bone-deep terror. She knew where surrender to him would lead. To a repetition of her parents' dismal pattern.

She'd grown up witnessing what misery could be wrought when involvement in a relationship was one-sided. Her mother's unrequited emotions toward her father had destroyed her mind, had led her—as Clarissa and her siblings believed—to end her life.

Not that she blamed her father. He'd done what he had to rule a kingdom. It had been her mother who'd been unable to understand the nature of their political marriage or accept it, who'd wanted to turn it into a love match and had only managed to drive her distant husband further away. Ferruccio was everything her father was—including whatever had driven her mother to destruction—a thousand times over.

The memory of her mother's life scared her enough to douse the insanity.

She started struggling in his arms, as if fighting for her life.

He stiffened for a long moment, unable to make up his mind whether her struggle was an attempt to get closer or away.

He finally grunted something and tore his lips away from hers, put her down.

Panting, every muscle spasming with the slow poison of the need he'd infected her with—a need that would eat through her if it went unappeased—she stumbled away, searching desperately for her equilibrium.

For a few seconds, the flames blazing on the poles surrounding her made her feel like an animal trapped within a circle of fire. As her mind rebooted, she realized how apt that fear was. She might not be physically trapped or in danger, but she was in every other way.

And her trapper—her hunter—was closing in on her again.

She squeezed her eyes shut, bit down on her lip, hard, to stop herself from turning around and throwing herself into his arms and letting him finish what he'd started.

His hands descended on her shoulders, pulled her back against him. She couldn't even tremble, could only lean back limply, exposing her neck for him to nuzzle. He took this as consent, again cupping her breast, her sex, rocking her against his arousal as he suckled her earlobe, whispered in her ear, "I didn't intend to go this far. But I touched you, and you responded and…"

She pushed out of his arms. This time he let her go at once. She finished rearranging her clothes, gave him a sullen look. "Sure, it's my fault, because I 'responded.'"

He shoved his hands into his pockets, drawing her eyes to the huge bulge in his pants. Her insides clenched. She swallowed. *Dio,* she was literally drooling over him.

"I'm not saying it's your fault. I'm saying I'm not proud that I set out to kiss you and almost ended up taking you. I never lose control like that, never surrender to the heat of the moment."

"No? Excuse me if I don't believe that, what with you being oversexed and overendowed, as well as overeverything else."

He looked incredulous. "You think I would have gotten where I am today if my libido had any say in my actions and decisions?"

"You're a man, aren't you? I'd say libido is the *only* thing that has a say in your decisions where women are concerned."

"Then you don't know much about men. Real ones, anyway. A man steered by his libido 'where women are concerned' is an immature dolt who ends up destroying what he achieves by making the wrong decisions at the wrong times for the wrong reasons."

"I happen to agree. So you're saying I made you lose your legendary control? Good one. Especially since you don't want me at all. This is just a hostile takeover for you."

He gave her a sweeping, lustful glance, huffed a short laugh. "You clearly have no concept of what *hostile* is. Or an inkling about what I'm like when I am. And if you think almost taking you standing up and becoming rock-hard whenever I so much as think of you isn't wanting you, I wonder if you even know the basics of the male sexual response."

"You're just aroused by the game you've been playing. You know, the one where you get to enforce your will on the only woman, it seems, who has ever said no to you."

A merciless gleam entered his eyes as his lips curled. "Your resistance always did infuriate me, when I sensed your answering desire. And now that I've felt how incendiary that desire is, and how it sets me on fire, if I wanted you to the factor of a thousand before, I now want you to that of a million. But even if it did get out of control, this explosive episode proved one thing. When I take you, Clarissa, it will be because you're begging me to."

She glared at him, hating him more for being so right about the magnitude of her desire. She had to vanquish it if she wanted to survive. "I wonder what level your arrogance can reach before you overdose on it. That would be a well-deserved end, not to mention an effective and fair solution to this mess. And before you gloat some more about how much I want you, that doesn't mean I'll act on it. I want to eat chocolate fudge day and night, but you won't see me giving in to the temptation any time in this life."

"But bingeing on me won't make you fat and sick. Giving in to the temptation of falling into my arms and bed will provide rigorous workouts that will keep you in perfect shape and health, and the calorie-free pleasure I'll saturate you with will make you realize you've been starving, make you wonder how you've lived so long with such deprivation."

She felt as if the whole world had become a tiny room, with its walls closing in on her. He was just too much, too powerful. Unstoppable. And when he turned coaxing, seductive, he was devastating. She couldn't resist him. And she had to.

There was only one way she could think of to stop him. Make him angry.

"Why don't you just drop the act? You only want me because I'm the king's daughter. That has always been my attraction, hasn't it? You've acquired everything else—God only knows how—but now the world has gone so crazy, *you* can become Castaldini's future king—and you still want to acquire me as the most suitable accessory to your impending royal status."

* * *

Ferruccio felt his heart turn to stone inside his chest.

He'd long believed she looked down on him because of the circumstances of his birth.

But not only had she now intimated that she believed he'd attained his wealth and power through criminal methods and that she still cringed at the idea of giving in to the desire that seethed like a bound beast between them, not only had she just confirmed his worst suspicions why, but she'd revealed that the situation was worse than he'd thought.

She thought he'd been pursuing her to acquire her lineage by association, still wanted it even now, to paint himself with her legitimacy. She didn't just think him a lowborn bastard but a sleazy social climber.

And she called *him* arrogant.

If he thought he'd enjoy punishing her for her arrogance before, he would now outright relish it. In every way imaginable.

He looked at her. Silky hair billowed around her shoulders like a caramel gold shroud of mystery in the night breeze. That body he'd almost lost his mind over was tense. He felt it emitting that tractor beam of attraction that had always drawn him inexorably. He'd always thought it had been the real her inside the body that had so attracted him. But no matter what he'd felt during the past few hours—that his belief had been more than validated—he'd been wrong.

Yet, he could still feel that body reverberating with the unassuaged need he'd sent storming through her. *That* he relished. If not as much as he did seeing that face of pure temptation pinched with worry. She must be wondering if she'd just made an irreversible mistake by baring her true opinion of him so blatantly.

She had no idea how right she was.

"As interesting as your opinions of my intentions are…" he gave her a smile that had had grown men sweating "…this… meeting is over, Clarissa. Now run along and go throw yourself in your father's loving arms and sob to him over your ordeal at the hands of the conceited, cruel man he threw you to like a human sacrifice. Let him soothe you and tell you exactly why you have to come back to me and beg me to take you."

Four

Clarissa went back to her father.

She was delivered back to him, more precisely. Just as Ferruccio had had her picked up like a package, he'd had her dropped back like one. His men had been implacable about carrying out his orders to the letter. He'd said to take her back to the king, and no matter how much she frothed with rage, they took her back to his very door. She'd barely managed to stop them from taking her to his bedside and have him sign a receipt for her.

She entered her father's apartments, shaking with chagrin, with the ever-expanding shock waves from every second she'd spent with Ferruccio, desperately hoping that everything he had told her had not been because he'd been certain of every word he'd said and of his damned hundred percent success rate.

She closed the door behind her, leaned on it and closed her eyes.

Finally. Some alone time. She needed to inject some semblance of calm and control into her thoughts, and hopefully in her expression and words, before entering her father's bedroom.

"Rissa, *mia cara figlia,* where have you been all night?"

She almost jumped out of her skin. Her father, who was so rarely out of bed these days, materialized at the passageway by the door she'd entered through.

Her frayed nerves snapped. "As if you don't know."

Pain stabbed dead center in her chest at her father's grimace of hurt surprise. She cursed Ferruccio with a new fervor. She'd never dreamed the day would come when she'd snap at her father like that. What made it even worse was that what once would have been a mere blink and tightening of lips had become a grotesque, one-sided distortion with the aftereffect of his stroke.

Her heart broke all over again at seeing the evidence of her once all-powerful father's incapacitation. For her to be the reason behind even a moment of his pain was unbearable.

Her heart thudded as she watched him drag his weakened leg, leaning heavily on his walking stick as he limped to the first chair in his reception area and collapsed heavily onto it.

He sat for a moment, not meeting her eyes, recovering from the few steps' effort, his breathing erratic. Then he finally rasped, "I knew only that you were meeting with Ferruccio earlier today."

"The meeting took longer than expected." She struggled not to let anger and bitterness taint her tone. She shouldn't let Ferruccio's words poison her against her father. She needed to hear how things stood from him before she made up her mind who to blame. "Do you know why he asked for me to be the one to negotiate with him?"

Her father exhaled. "If you've learned anything about Ferruccio, Rissa, you must know he never declares his reasons to anyone. But I had theories."

She tensed. "And those were?"

"He's…interested in you. He always has been."

All tension drained out of her as if with a punch to the gut. "And yet you sent me to him."

"Why are you so angry, Rissa?" Alarm suddenly entered her father's steel-blue eyes. "Did he…upset you?"

"That would be the understatement of the year."

Alarm was swept aside on a tide of fury. For a moment, Clarissa could see once again the formidable man and king who'd ruled for forty years, who'd made Castaldini a piece of heaven on earth for almost thirty of those. "What did he do? Tell me."

As if she would. She waved it away. "What's important here is that you knew he wasn't interested in my professional acumen. Why did you send me to him when you knew he had a personal agenda?"

"Why would you be so against that?" Typical. He never answered questions, always volleyed one back. "I never understood why you were so…reticent with him. I thought it might be a good time to settle this. He'll become my crown prince and your future king. And I wasn't against the possibility of him becoming even more."

As in her groom. Her skull suddenly felt too small for her brain. "So you thought the opportunity to indulge in some matchmaking had presented itself?"

"What father doesn't take every opportunity to try to see to his daughter's happiness?"

"And you thought Ferruccio, of all people, was the way to mine?"

"Who else could be, but someone like him?"

"There's *no one* like him."

"My point precisely."

"Dio, Padre…" The lament of how deluded his belief was recoiled in her chest as a terrible suspicion descended on her.

What if this was some side effect of his illness? He'd told her he'd been forgetting things, had been unable to focus. What if this skewed thought he'd formed of Ferruccio as her Prince Charming was a delusion he was suffering from? Brought on by his brush with mortality, his current condition? What if he was scared to die and leave her alone, and he'd latched onto Ferruccio as guardian-angel material based on his power and affluence? Maybe fueled by Ferruccio's expression of interest in her? Or maybe he'd gotten wind of Ferruccio's pursuit of her and built this imaginary scenario around it?

If that was the case, she should let it go. How could she possibly berate him for wanting the best for her, blame him for trying to see to it the best way he thought he could?

It didn't matter, anyway. What mattered was the real catastrophe Ferruccio had so coldly informed her was in progress.

She inhaled. "Is it true? Is Castaldini in danger?"

Her father blinked. "Ferruccio told you that?"

"Please tell me he was at least exaggerating."

"I don't know what he told you." He averted his gaze as he said that. And she knew that every word Ferruccio had told her was true. "But maybe it's time for me to tell you the truth."

"Maybe? *Dio Santo,* why did you even think you should hide it from me at all? *Padre,* I'm a grown-up, PhD-holding professional, I've been elected a Council member by the people. How could you possibly keep something of this magnitude from me? How did you even manage it, when it seems everyone else knows?"

His lips twisted. His condition leant the grimace even more irony. "I may not be the king I once was, but my word still carries some weight. I demanded that no one tell you."

She'd start tearing her hair out any second now. *"Why?"*

"Because no matter how much you've grown, how strong you've become, you're still my little girl, Rissa. Because all of Castaldini's troubles are my fault, and I couldn't bring myself to tell you how big a mess your father has made of everything. I hoped I could fix it, and never have to admit it to you and see disillusion or disappointment in your eyes."

Her tears gushed. She threw herself at his feet and hugged him around his waist with all her strength, sobs tearing out of her as she burrowed her face in his chest the way she had countless times during her tumultuous childhood, when he'd been the impenetrable fortress she'd taken refuge in. "You'll never see either in my eyes, *Padre.* You'll always be my hero."

He tried to hug her back, managing to apply real pressure

only with his healthy arm, the other one barely capable of smoothing her hair a couple of times before the tremors of weakness made him drop it to his side.

They remained like that, locked in the cocoon of their soul-deep connection, the king kissing the top of her head and crooning to her the soothing endearments and the unconditional love that had once been the sole thing that had made her safe enough to sleep, brave enough to live.

Then he began to talk. "It began about ten years ago. I started to lose my perspective in external affairs, to slack off in internal ones. I made many enemies within Castaldini, making it easy for outside enemies to find openings through which to infiltrate our land, take a foothold. I am guilty of glossing over too much, hiding it from all but the highest ranks of Council members. Then I had my stroke. To the world, to the people of Castaldini, the only serious thing seemed to be the market crash, but that is only the tip of the iceberg of problems. I know what you'll say, that Leandro and Durante are dealing with the financial situation, that things seem stable now.

"But it's the calm before the storm. With Leandro and Durante regents only, with me still the king, a crisis is inevitable. Without a formidable crown prince and future king, it's a matter of time before the internal decay weakens the kingdom, until it collapses under the pressures applied by the nations vying to assimilate our resources to feed their expanding needs. Only Leandro and Durante have enough power to stop that temporarily, but they both declined the crown. For the best of reasons, I admit. In their positions now, they'd stave off many immediate dangers, but only a king can have the long-term influence to do it permanently. Ferruccio is the only one left who has the power needed, both financially and politically, to maintain Castaldini's sovereignty."

Clarissa lay on her bed staring at the ceiling, waiting for the wave to crash.

Next second, like clockwork, it did.

She shook with it, the fury that had been wreaking havoc on her since she'd left her father's apartments last night.

She hadn't slept a wink, had risen from her bed as dawn stretched its first fingers across the sky and paced her room for hours. It was 10:00 a.m. now, and she felt exhausted, beaten.

Castaldini *was* in clear and present danger.

When she'd realized in how much danger the kingdom was in, she'd raved and ranted that her father should draft either Leandro or Durante to the duty, that they weren't entitled to refuse when stakes were that catastrophic. But he'd told her why either Leandro or Durante would still end Castaldini as they knew it—Leandro by his incompatible political views, and Durante by bringing an end to the very law around which Castaldini had been built.

She'd struggled to enumerate the measures that could be installed so that either man's reign wouldn't do the predicted damage, but her father had countered every one with an undeniable projection of how it would fail. He'd told her that, before she'd become part of it, the Council had discussed everything in dozens of raging closed sessions, until they had admitted there was no other way out. Did she think anything less could have made them reach the decision to make the offer to Ferruccio?

So this was it. It *was* down to Ferruccio. It was up to him to save Castaldini. He was, in every way, the only one who could.

And that *bastard*—and the epithet had absolutely nothing to do with his birth, but with his character, his behavior—cared nothing about it. He cared only about getting his way. He wanted his "incentive." *Her.*

She'd once thought him a god. He lived up to the belief in many ways. He now did in the most maddening way of all. To save king and country, she had to offer herself at the altar of the vicious deity he'd turned out to be.

She twisted around in bed, reached across to her nightstand, picked up her cell phone.

Time to discuss the terms of her sacrifice.

She pushed the buttons. The private number he said only a handful were privileged enough to have. She'd never called it before. She'd memorized it the first time he'd given it to her, with the second invitation she refused. She was in no position to refuse him…anything…anymore. As he'd said she would be.

The line clicked open before the first ring ended.

He'd been waiting for her. Figured.

She waited for him to speak. To gloat. But there was only a protracted moment of absolute silence on the other end.

He was waiting for her to initiate the second and final round.

Good luck with that, as he'd said. She was holding her breath as she did to get rid of hiccups. She had this ridiculous conviction that if she held it long enough, she'd get rid of this whole nightmare. Yeah, right. By passing out, maybe.

At last *he* breathed, the sound of his inhalation, then slow exhalation pooling warm moistness at the juncture of her legs. And that was before he murmured darkly, intimately, "Clarissa."

She covered the mouthpiece with her hand and almost coughed out the air that would have ruptured her lungs if she'd held it in another second. *Just get it over with.*

She drew in a hasty breath then blurted it out along with the question that had been eating at her. "What did you mean by 'taking' me with the crown? You want to marry me, right?"

A bark of cruelly masculine laughter ricocheted inside her skull. "*Marry* you? Without a long, hard test drive?"

She shut her eyes. How did he do it? How did every word he uttered blind her with arousal even as it also did with anger?

"So you want to have an affair first?" she seethed.

A shorter laugh revved through the ether to buzz through her every bone. "It might be an affair *only*. You might dissatisfy me, and it would end there."

She counted to ten. "If you'll be satisfied with an affair, considering the situation, as you've so…kindly said, I have no option but to accept. But I need to set parameters up-front."

He tsked. "Parameters? How businesslike of you. Highly inappropriate, when you're discussing the plunge into sensual decadence I had planned."

She jerked onto her back, tremors coalescing into one violent shudder before she went still and tense all over. "Had? Does that mean you've changed your mind?"

He let her reach screaming pitch before he said, "I have."

She almost felt her components scatter apart with the sudden loss of the tension that had been holding her together. The cacophony of emotion that rushed to fill the void was a deafening mixture.

Relief yelled loudest. Thankfulness mumbled its grudging concession. But to her disbelieving chagrin, it was disappointment that somehow made its whimpers heard over everything else.

It seemed he'd paused, knowing that these reactions would prey on her. His next words made that clear—made them all redundant. "I've changed my mind about what you deserve."

She gritted her teeth. "Meaning?"

"Meaning that for six years, you must remember with crystal clarity, I've given you the courtesy of being the pursued. But I've decided that you've forfeited your right to such consideration."

"And in your infinite wisdom, what did you decide I deserve?"

"That you must get down from your high tower and do all the running from now on. After all, you're a record-holding champion at it."

"If that means you'll be running ahead, there's nothing I'd love more than to run after you until you drop."

She knew his smile turned to its most wicked. The illicit excitement that thrummed through her told her so. "No danger of that. I'm not as fast as you are, but my stamina is legendary."

And the terrible thing was that she knew he was stating facts. He wasn't a self-deceiving braggart like so many men she'd heard making such pompous claims. He was a man who knew his worth, his powers, and made no pretense at false modesty. A man who'd survived and triumphed over obstacles and dangers, over horrors she couldn't begin to imagine. He also had the most glamorous women in the world fighting for a place on his one-night-stand waiting list. She'd bet he had stamina by the freight-load.

She harumphed. "So you'll employ that Herculean stamina to stay one step ahead as I play 'pursuer' this time around. Any rules to this game I should be aware of? Any points to be scored? Any ultimate goal? Or is this going to be a wild swine chase?"

His chuckles rose at her insult. He loved it when she played rough, didn't he? Who knew he had a masochistic streak. But then, it made sense. A steady diet of simpering obedience and syrupy adulation must make him sick to his stomach. What better than the corrosive sourness of her irreverence to equalize the queasiness?

If that was the case, he'd be happy to know she had verbal abuse by the truckload to pour over his arrogant head.

Meanwhile, *he* poured the black magic of his amusement directly into her brain. "As long as you keep the wild part of that chase going, this…swine will let you get as creative as you like about the rules. Points are scored at my discretion, of course. As for the ultimate goal, it's changing my mind. You see, I'm no longer convinced you're a…good enough incentive. Your mission, should you choose to accept it, is to convince me otherwise."

"Any tips about how I'm supposed to achieve mission impossible?" She injected as much poison as she could into the sweetness of her tone.

His voice deepened. "If you succeed in making me spontaneously combust, that would be a good start."

"And a fitting end."

He hooted with laughter. She shuddered, pressed her thighs together, trying to ameliorate the throbbing ache deep between them. "Go ahead, give me your best shot."

"I'd rather do my worst. Pity you're dozens of miles away."

"Are you alone?"

His sudden question aborted the flow of her venom, yanked sexual awareness to the forefront. "Y-yes…."

"Where?"

"I-in my bedroom."

"Describe it for me."

She tossed a frantic look around. "Uh…it's big. Huge."

"Details, woman."

"You've been inside the palace. You know the dimensions and the general style of an average room here."

"Your bedroom isn't an average room. And I haven't been…inside it. Yet."

She latched on the first part of his statement, skirted the provocative part like she would a land mine. "Actually, it's way below average."

"Explain." She cursed herself for getting into that, fell silent. He growled, "*Bene.* Be prepared for an inspection visit."

"I thought I was supposed to pursue you now."

"My visit will be in pursuit of answers, not your delectable body."

"My room is a mess, okay?" she blurted out.

"You're untidy?" She heard his surprise, then his disbelief. "Even if you are, you have a dozen ladies-in-waiting cleaning up after you."

"I'm not a paragon of personal organization," she hissed. "But if you think I'm allowed to be 'untidy,' just because I'm a princess, maybe you haven't met Antonia, my *bambinàia.*"

"I have. A formidable woman. Is she still your nanny?"

"I call her nanny, but don't you think I've outgrown the need for one? She's my so-called lady-in-waiting now, but she's more like a mother to me. And not only hasn't her job description as my nanny ever included picking up after me, but her method of turning little girls into princesses was something close to what the U.S. Special Forces use in training Navy SEALs."

Silence expanded after her words died away. Then he inhaled. "So you haven't been pampered and coddled, *mia bella unica?*"

She swallowed past the sudden barbed tightness in her throat.

That kindness. When she'd thought it an impossibility. It was probably her imagination. Maybe a glitch in the line.

But she hadn't imagined him calling her his unique beauty. "Your view of my life isn't just rosy, it's fluorescent fuchsia."

She expected him to laugh his hardest this time. And again, he did the last thing she expected him to do.

His tone became a gentle stroke, smoothing her frayed nerves, soothing her rawness. "I stand corrected. But your parents have a lot to answer for. You were born for pampering and coddling."

She almost snorted. "No, thank you. I'm glad they didn't agree with you. I would have grown up a thoughtless, useless brat."

"Pampering and coddling don't have to mean spoiling. Used right, by firm, loving parents, they can be fortifying, nurturing, stabilizing. There's nothing better to contribute to the development of a balanced character and the maintenance of a healthy psyche."

She almost blurted out *And what would you know about that?*

She burrowed back into the mattress with relief that the words hadn't exited her lips. He would have taken them in the worst way possible, and she would have felt even worse.

She meant only to marvel at his insight into something he hadn't experienced. But then again, she shouldn't wonder. His uncanny knowledge of the mechanisms that made humans tick was behind his almost frightening success.

He was going on. "But your parents decided it the best course of action to be tough on you, so instead of a thoughtless, useless brat, you've grown up a merciless, shameless siren."

After another silent beat, she sat up. "Hello? Are you taking another call? Shall I wait on the line until you finish talking to whomever it is you just called all those far-fetched things?"

"You see? Shameless." Before she could answer, he went on. "But since you're not untidy, why is your room a mess?"

Dio, the man forgot nothing, couldn't be distracted. Figured.

She gave in. "Because it hasn't seen a coat of paint in over fifteen years. Name any sign you can imagine of long neglect in such an old building, and it's here. Distintegrating wood paneling, leaking ceiling and peeling paint, just to mention the surface stuff."

An edge entered his voice. "The rest of the palace is in good condition. How is it possible your living quarters haven't been given priority in maintenance and renovations?"

"My living quarters aren't part of the national monument area of the palace."

"You're the princess of Castaldini." He sounded indignant.

"You should see the king's quarters."

The silence lengthened beyond her ability to bear it this time. Especially when she could almost hear that warp-speed mind of his streaking to conclusions. It was another thing to prove how much Castaldini needed him.

At last he inhaled. Then, after a long pause, slowly exhaled. The nuances of the sounds didn't transmit male awareness and triumph this time, but contemplation, deliberation, and if she could possibly believe it, thoughtfulness, consideration. It seemed her sensory capacity had converged on her sense of hearing. She was picking up more through his breathing and tones than from his words. And whether she was picking up right or wrong, it moved her, messed up her insides. Then—of course—he made it far worse.

"What are you wearing, Clarissa?"

His whisper, the total unexpectedness of the question, made her heart skip over a few beats like a little girl would over squares in hopscotch. She wet her aching, parched lips. "Clothes."

"Really? Whatever happened to fig leaves?" Her lips twitched. How did he engage her sense of humor, when she wanted to murder him? "What do you sleep in?"

"What *do* people sleep in? But I'm no longer in my pajamas."

"You're not 'people.' And if I become the future king of Castaldini, I'll issue a royal decree prohibiting you from wearing pajamas. A body like yours shouldn't be encased in anything but drapes of chiffon, wraps of tulle, veils of gauze. Or just jewelry."

"Sure. Just the things to attend Council meetings in," she scoffed. "Fig leaves would be preferable."

"You haven't answered my question again, Clarissa."

She sighed. "In the interest of preventing an inspection visit—I'm wearing another nondescript skirt suit."

"Nothing you put on your body remains nondescript. After last night, skirt suits have entered the realm of highly erotic garments. Following the same rationalization, pajamas on you are probably the height of sexiness." If he thought she had anything to say to that, he could think again. She was busy dealing with the impending heart attack he'd so casually caused. But he didn't wait for her commentary. "What are you wearing beneath the jacket? Is your top buttoned, or pulled on, like the one you had on yesterday?"

"I don't see—"

"It's I who wants to see. In my mind's eye. Now, do as I tell you. Take off your jacket. Slowly."

His whispers, hypnotic, incendiary, were dragging her down into an endless well of mindlessness, incinerating rules and logic and memory. She still struggled. "Ferruccio, I don't think—"

"Don't think. Do it. This is where you start convincing me again. The jacket, Clarissa. Off."

She took the phone away from her ear, stared at it, wondering if it had turned into a device that was whispering delusions. She put it back on, gritted, "It's off."

His whisper grew hotter, darker. "Liar."

"How do you know if I'm lying or not?" She struggled not to pant. "Do you have my room bugged? Am I on camera now?"

"I can tell from your tone, from your breathing. From every cell in my body that's telling me you're still covered in layers of clothes. And you haven't answered me. Buttons or pulled-on?"

"B-buttons…" she stammered.

"Leave the jacket on then. For now. Unbutton your blouse for me, Clarissa. Start at the top." This time her hands trembled to obey him, as if powered by his will, his impatience. "Stop at the button just below your breasts." She did. "Turn your phone to speaker mode. I want both your hands free." She did that, too. "Now cross your hands inside your blouse, *bellissima.* Knead your breasts, then flick your nails over your nipples through your bra." She fell back on the bed again, did as he instructed. "They're hard now. Aching. Begging for my fingers, my lips and tongue and teeth." And they were. How they were. "Do you remember the pressure I applied when I nipped them? Pinch them as hard." She did, gasped, arched off the bed. "Again." And again she did it, and every time he prodded her.

Fire raged through her. Her brain was sizzling, her chest, her eyes steaming, the heat in her gut converging to pour between her thighs, the pounding there beating to the frantic rhythm of her heart. She felt as if he'd taken over her body, was using her own hands as extensions of his lust, as if he was the one doing these things to her again. As he was. Whoever said the mind was the most powerful sex organ had been right. And he'd taken over hers.

"Pull your skirt up, touch your buttocks as I did, squeeze them." She obeyed, unable to suppress her whimpers anymore. "It's me doing it, pulling you against my erection, grinding into you. Spread your legs, Clarissa, let me have better access, open yourself and take more of me."

She opened herself, could swear she felt him bearing down on her, the throbbing where he said he was, but wasn't, becoming erratic with her heart's short-circuiting rhythm.

"Now, do what you wanted me to do—what I would have done if you didn't stop me. Cup yourself, Clarissa, tight. You're burning now." She was. And she couldn't bear it. "Slip your hand inside your panties, spread your lips open. Now slide your fingers through your flowing nectar." She did, keened, trembling on the edge now. His voice thickened, became harsh as gravel. "You're melting, empty, losing your mind, unable to breathe with the hunger. I can see you, Clarissa, quaking on the edge of release. I can scent your need. I can feel your heart stampeding, your body tautening, your core demanding me."

He stopped, drew in a shuddering breath.

Her lips trembled on a smile. He was as affected as she was, as distressed. His breath, when it rushed out, felt as if it filled her, the stimulus that almost tipped her over. She waited, needing it to be his words that did.

"But this stops here, *mia magnifica.* Anything more, you'll have to come get it."

Everything stilled, froze. The world. Her body. Her heart.

"I'm flying back to Castaldini as we speak." His voice was crisp and distant all of a sudden, all intensity and intimacy evaporated. "I had to tend to some business, but I'll be back in my mansion within the hour. You've gone a long way toward convincing me. I expect you to continue your…persuasion, then."

Five

It was hours before Clarissa made herself leave her bed.

The first hour, she could barely move, think, breathe.

The frustration, the humiliation, had been paralyzing, suffocating. She'd tried to escape into oblivion. And to her enormous surprise, she succeeded. It seemed her nervous system had taken all it could, had done the one thing that would spare her real and lasting damage—shut down.

She woke up disoriented, sobbing.

More hours passed while she tried to regain semblance of equilibrium. She'd stood beneath scalding water and tried to let it wash away her confusion and anger—and most of all, the insidious craving Ferruccio had infused in her blood, the memory of those moments when he'd remote-controlled her, driven her to the brink of insanity, before withdrawing and leaving her feeling like she'd never stop falling. The next hour was spent going through the motions of drying her hair and getting dressed—and not in a skirt suit. Then she'd sat down at her computer table and finally let herself think. Let the one thought that now filled her being take the form of words.

She didn't want to see or hear of Ferruccio ever again.

But she had to.

He'd demanded that she report to his mansion.

And she'd made her decision.

This ended tonight.

She'd tell him where he could stick his demands and terms. She was done being more fuel for his planetary-size ego. If he wanted to to punish her, and appease said ego, she'd assure him, he'd dealt her a blow that should satisfy him for the rest of his unnatural life. Then she would show him why he couldn't refuse to be Castaldini's crown prince, what was in it for him. So many things that didn't include her. She'd *persuade* him, all right. To leave her out of the bargain and still go ahead with it.

With that fortifying hope powering her, she sprang into action.

The moment she left her apartments, Antonia descended on her like a disapproving mother eagle.

"Clarissa, can you tell me what exactly you're trying to do here? Signore Selvaggio's envoys arrived *ten hours ago,* saying you have an appointment with him!"

"And you didn't swoop down on me the minute they arrived? That must be the minute hell froze over."

"I did swoop down, many times. You were dead to the world. In your clothes. I gave up hours ago."

"Take heart. It must have been that final trial that succeeded in yanking me out of my stupor."

"What's wrong with you, Clarissa? You sound…intoxicated."

Clarissa barked a mirthless laugh. "You know what? I think you're absolutely right, since intoxication happens when something rises in the blood to the level of toxicity."

The woman looked as if she'd said the sun was checkered purple and blue. "You're saying you've been consuming alcohol…or something even worse?"

Clarissa smirked. "I'd say arrogance and testosterone are definitely worse."

Antonia looked to be at a total loss. "I've never seen you in this condition, Clarissa. Are you really sick? Or are you just trying to gloss over the fact that you disregarded an appointment with a man of Signore Selvaggio's importance?"

Clarissa gave her a serene look. "Hey, I'm just fashionably late. That's a woman's prerogative, isn't it?"

The raven-haired, green-eyed battleship of a woman, whom Clarissa loved dearly, dragon ferocity and military discipline and all, tutted. "You're inexcusably, *obscenely* late. And you're not 'a woman,' You're a princess."

"Believe me, *bambinàia,* right now I wish I wasn't either. I'm in this damned situation because of those damned double X chromosomes and that damned accident of birth."

"What 'damned situation' is that? I hope you don't mean having someone of Signore Selvaggio's caliber interested in you."

"First my father, now you. And no doubt I'll find out everyone knows of his so-called interest in me. And it seems you're all thrilled about it. I wonder why none of you ever told me that?"

"I've spent six years wondering how you could possibly be not falling all over yourself to return his interest."

"And you didn't try to bulldoze me into seeing the error of my ways? Shock and awe!"

"That's the one thing I took it upon myself never to try to influence you in, Clarissa." Clarissa met her nanny's shrewd eyes, saw the sadness there. She was talking about Clarissa's mother, to whom Antonia had been lady-in-waiting since she was eighteen, twelve years before she'd become Clarissa's nanny. Antonia was the one who'd witnessed how Angelica, Clarissa's mother, had been influenced to marry her father for business and political reasons, how the wrong reasons for marriage had never amounted to a healthy relationship and had ended up destroying the queen. Antonia finally sighed. "And then, it's been a long time since you've needed my guidance in anything."

A surge of love and emotion welled up in Clarissa. She hugged Antonia, needing the assuagement of her sturdy body and spirit, the impenetrable haven of her embrace. "As if that ever stopped you, *bambinàia.*"

After a moment of hugging her back, Antonia pushed her away. "You're right. I'll always be an overbearing, interfering woman where it comes to you, the jewel I spent a good chunk of my life polishing and protecting, the daughter I didn't bear, who is now the one thing that brings joy to my heart after I lost my Benito. So here's some more unsolicited guidance. This Selvaggio man is the one for whom I will break my rule of non-interference in your future choices where men are concerned. Stop being a fool, girl. Snatch him up."

"Ah, *bambinàia,* you really have no idea who he is, do you?"

"If you mean that he's an illegitimate D'Agostino, yes, I do."

Clarissa coughed an incredulous laugh. "Seems I was the last to know that, too. But that's not what I meant. I meant his character, his nature."

"He's the most complex man I've ever met. And that's what makes him the right one for you."

"If you mean that because I'm such a multifaceted character myself, thanks for the implied praise. I think. But the problem with such a labyrinthine man is that, among the qualities you admire, you find others to abhor. He might be godlike in looks and personal influence, in success and power, but he's also arrogant, driven and cruelly ambitious."

Antonia gave her a considering look. "Hmm. Arrogant, you say? I've seen only evidence to the contrary. All those exquisite invitations he sent you that I found in the bin, torn apart as if they had tainted your hands. Besides being confounded by your reaction, I know that an arrogant man would have taken one such rejection and never again given you the time of day."

Clarissa's lips twisted. "That's where 'driven' and 'cruelly ambitious' come into play. Ferruccio Selvaggio pursues his target until it drops of exhaustion in his lap."

"So that's your evasive maneuver? Going to him, not when he demanded, but when you deem to, half a day later?" Antonia scowled. "You were free to act as you wished when it was a personal matter, Clarissa, but this meeting is official business. After the way you treated him in the past, any other man would have called the king and Council and filed a formal complaint against you. Frankly, that he hasn't, makes me admire him more."

"So why don't *you* go to him?" Clarissa snapped, and immediately burned in embarrassment at the look that devolved her into a ten-year-old. She shook it off, went on determinedly. "He should be thankful I'm going at all. If this meeting didn't have 'official business' squished in between his personal agenda, he would have never gotten the chance to be in the same square mile I'm in. And if any woman can be late, surely a princess can get away with being inexcusably, obscenely late."

Antonia raised one eyebrow at her. "When did you get a personality transplant?"

Clarissa shrugged. "It's a personality that sprouts up at the mere mention of Ferruccio Selvaggio-slash-D'Agostino."

Antonia gave her suspicious look. "You're playing the spoilt princess, trying to drive him away, aren't you?" She stopped, her eyes rounding, as if she'd just realized the secret of the universe. "*Dio Santo!* How didn't I see this before? You're not *interested* in him, you're *crazy* about him!"

There was no use trying to pull the wool over the eyes of the woman who'd practically raised her. It *was* astounding that Antonia hadn't realized the true nature of her feelings for Ferruccio till now. Seemed she was a better actress than she'd thought. "And I'd be crazier if I did 'snatch him up.'"

For the first time in twenty-eight-years' worth of memory, Clarissa witnessed the sight of Antonia dumbstruck. After a long moment of gaping at her open-mouthed, Antonia shook her head. "*Si,* it's true. I have absolutely nothing to say at the moment. I'm speechless. I'll probably overcompensate later, but for now, go ahead. Either apologize to his envoys and reschedule, or go to the meeting and try to explain the hefty *oops* of a ten-hour delay. Or just do him the courtesy you've been doing for six years. Turn him down and be done with it. You've had plenty of practice after all. Or…no, scratch that. I have no clue. This situation isn't complex, it's incomprehensible."

Clarissa gave a sarcastic huff. "Even when you don't get something, you always end up summing it up perfectly."

Antonia turned and walked away, still shaking her head. Clarissa duly went to Ferruccio's envoys.

They again escorted her to the royal airport to board the jet he'd sent to collect her. During the twenty-minute flight and the drive on landing, she was accompanied by the man who'd met her last night at the airport and had driven her to Ferruccio's mansion. From the few words she managed to extract from him she found out he was Alfredo, Ferruccio's valet and personal assistant.

She got the distinct feeling that this thin, tall, hawkeyed man hated her.

Upon arriving at the mansion, he again walked her to the door and let her in. As he retreated, she detained him.

"Would you please tell him I'm here? I have to see him right away. This shouldn't take long, and then you can drive me back to the jet."

The man looked pointedly at the hand grasping his forearm, cleared his throat. "I'm sorry, *Principessa,* but I am under strict orders. Signore Selvaggio specifically said that whenever you arrive, you are to be let in and that everyone should retreat to their quarters off the estate until he orders us back."

Just as she'd thought yesterday. How convenient. To get her alone, to be free to do whatever he liked without worrying about witnesses. The only wagging tongues this would provoke would be those lashing at her, his latest conquest.

"If he's forbidden you to be on the premises with me here, please call him." He gave her an impassive look. She summoned every iota of control and princesslike graciousness she'd ever have drummed into her, let out a calming exhalation. "I couldn't tell him I was on my way, since his phone was turned off. But you must know how to contact him."

"Signore Selvaggio contacts me. I never intrude on him."

"This is no intrusion. He's expecting me."

"He *was* expecting you. Twelve hours ago."

So that was it. The man who seemed to despise her with a passion, was punishing her for daring to stand up his god!

"Well, I'm here now. How will he know that I am? How do I know he's even here anymore? He could be out doing one of those night sports he told me about."

"I have no idea, *Principessa.* He didn't inform me of his movements tonight. I regret that I can't help you. It's really up to you, what you do now. You can wait until he turns on his phone and you can inform him of your presence. Or he might come in if he's outside, or come downstairs if he's in the mansion. Or if you wish, I can escort you back to the jet and you can reschedule and return some other time."

All graciousness evaporated on a spike of frustration. "It isn't as if you're selling top-secret info to his rivals. *Dio!* So he gave you an order to let me in and leave. That applies only if he's waiting for me. But, because of my…tardiness…he's no longer doing so. So he won't consider you locating him to inform him of my presence a breach of his orders." Alfredo just looked back at her stonily. Clearly, he'd said his last word. And had driven her to the very tip of her wits' end. "Is he so indiscriminating in what he considers insubordination and so unreasonable in meting out punishment that he has you cowering in terror? If he is, then my father and the Council have it all wrong in thinking such a despot can possibly be king material."

The man seemed to expand with affront. "It is Your Highness who has it all wrong. It isn't fear that motivates anyone who works for Signore Selvaggio. It's allegiance. We strive to live up to his expectations, as he always surpasses ours."

Clarissa gaped at the man.

Whoa. Now that was an impassioned little speech. And no doubt the man had meant every word.

Figured. Hadn't Ferruccio himself told her how he manipulated people, had them writhing in contentment under his influence? If his conquests were ecstatic to be conquered by him, as she'd proved to be herself, what would his aides and employees feel? They must believe they were blessed to be chosen to serve in his pantheon, smiled upon by his approval. Just great.

She let the man go, watched him close the door behind him, feeling a cloud of resignation settle over her shoulders.

Which didn't serve any purpose. Alfredo was probably right.

Ferruccio was bound to come back. Or down. Or something.

Or nothing. That was what had happened for the next hour.

Ferruccio hadn't appeared. And now she was certain he wouldn't. He was punishing her for being late. The bastard.

She could excuse his right-hand man for being disdainful of her actions, since he didn't know the particulars. But for Ferruccio to dare think she would have rushed over here, after what he'd done to her! And he'd fooled even Antonia, the woman with the character-fathoming X-ray powers, into thinking he was such an outstanding and worthy man. Not that it mattered now. She had to sort through her options about how to deal with this situation.

Alfredo had given her only two options. Wait. Or leave.

Waiting was clearly a futile endeavor. Ferruccio would probably leave her stewing till morning, would maybe even leave the island without letting her see him. Leaving wasn't an option, either. It would draw this out to one, or many more, rounds.

She needed this to be over tonight.

Which brought her to a third option. Go looking for him.

She'd start by combing the upper floors. He was probably sitting in some office upstairs, watching her chase her tail on hidden surveillance cameras.

According to her exploration of the ground floor, there were three staircases leading to different places of the complexly designed mansion. One led to the tower, another to what comprised the eastern facade, the last to the western one.

Without stopping to consider where to start, she found her feet moving. Only after the compulsion had her scaling the stairs did she recall something he told her last night, during those magical hours by the sea. He said he'd insisted on changing the orientation of this place before building commenced. He'd said he was at his clearest, at his most tranquil and powerful, when he slept and worked facing west. That was where she was heading. That was where he was.

With every step up the stairs, her breath shortened. She was far from winded, but that premonition that had told her where she'd find him also told her she was walking into a new plane of existence. One she'd never exit the same, if at all.

She reached the mezzanine-level gallery where he'd stood looking down at her yesterday. From there, the western wing converged into two areas. She didn't hesitate, took the left passageway into a wide corridor of arched columnns.

At regular intervals between the arches about a foot above her head, triangular, bronze sconces, with their apex down and their bases up and open, radiated muted, golden lights across the stone walls, deepening the textures and casting shadows on every structure, boosting the impression that this was an ancient place that had been transported, intact, through time.

At the blind end of the corridor, a smaller replica of the mansion's main door was centered in a thirty-foot wall.

As she approached it, her upheaval rose until it shook her, deafened her.

She stumbled on the last step, ended up with the side of her face plastered to the cool oak. And then she heard them.

Rumbles. Dark, deep.

Agonized.

She froze, held her breath, attempted to silence her heart, strained to catch every nuance, fathom it.

Dio, why was he groaning like that? The terrible sounds quaked through her as explanations streaked through her mind. Suddenly one screeched to a halt, freezing her tremors with horror.

He could be with a woman. Or more than one. She could be hearing the sounds of him in the throes of passion.

The suspicion lasted seconds before conviction vaporized it.

No. He sounded like he was in *pain.*

Suddenly he went silent.

She barged into the room, her heart pounding.

The expansive room was dimly illuminated by sconces similar to those in the corridor. She'd taken two dozen leaps before her momentum died on the beige-marble floor. She came to a stumbling halt a few feet from what must have been a nine-by-nine bed, draped in darkness at the far end of the room.

And there he was, in its middle, spread out on his back. One muscled arm was thrown over his head, the other stretched at a right angle to his body. His formidable chest was bare, his hips and part of his slightly parted, endless legs twisted in dark sheets the color of which she couldn't fathom. His head was tipped back, his face turned toward an arched verandah door framed by white, translucent curtains that billowed in the balmy night breeze.

He looked like a decadent god in the depths of slumber.

But he was totally still. He didn't seem to be breathing.

Panic wrenched through her, propelled her to his side, breath and heartbeats shattering inside her chest.

Before she crashed beside him on the bed, ready to grab and shake him and sob for him to wake up, to be all right, he stirred.

She almost fell to the floor on her knees under the weight of overwhelming relief. *Dio, Dio, grazie, grazie* filled her head. He was…he was…just sleeping.

But he wasn't just sleeping.

Horror seeped back into her blood as she watched his face contort, jerked with the sound his teeth made as they gnashed into a silent snarl, as his whole body tensed.

His every muscle bulged as he arched up from the bed. His

veins, distended as if under a high-pressure surge, stood out like thick ropes running across his sweaty, sculpted flesh. Even in the dim light she could see his golden bronze color become livid with the rush of blood. His breathing turned explosive, erratic. The bed started to shake with the terrible tension arcing through him.

It was as if he were having a seizure. No, worse. It was as if he were struggling to escape a weight that was dragging him under, or crushing him. As if he were bracing for unendurable torture, suppressing agony so that it wouldn't escape his lips in vocal suffering. Then it did.

The rumbles seemed to originate from the deepest reaches of his soul before seeping through his body, guttural snarls filled with fury and ferocity, with dread and desperation, before they burst from his throat in growls of pure torment.

He was in the grips of an inescapable nightmare. Like the ones that still haunted her. The ones she'd assured everyone she no longer had. She'd learned to live with her chronic sleep invaders, trained herself to recognize their advent, to ward off their damage, to escape their talons. At least after she'd woken up. They came far and few between now, but seemed to have gained in power for being less frequent, as if each one slowly built to a crescendo before being unleashed on her unguarded psyche.

She recognized the same anguish radiating from him now, a frequency of distress that resonated with her own.

Was this a one-time occurrence, or was it recurring?

It *was* recurring. She recognized the signs. So, what pain and horror did he relive every time he closed his eyes, surrendered to the supposedly healing embrace of sleep?

The unending possibilities seared her imagination, all the things that could have scarred him body and soul as he grew up, things of which she knew she'd never have anywhere near an accurate picture of their damage and cruelty.

She thought he'd survived them all unscathed. She'd thought him invulnerable.

He wasn't. And here was the proof. This was a man writhing

in torment so deep, suffering from wounds so indelible, they made anything she'd ever endured laughable.

Empathy flooded through her, drove her to her knees beside him on the bed. Her heart would burst if she didn't reach out to him, try to save him from the fangs of the darkness festering inside him, preying on him. She'd do anything to tear him away from its ugliness, absorb all she could into herself. And if some distant voice said this was her nemesis, her tormentor, she willfully ignored its insidious warnings.

This was the only man who'd ever aroused her emotions and passions. Now he aroused every compassionate, protective fiber within her. She couldn't bear the thought of his pain. Not him. Not her conquering, indomitable Ferruccio.

She leaned forward, touched her lips to his clenched eyelids, one after the other, placed her shaking palms on his chest, exerted as gentle a pressure as she could to defuse the excess electricity of upheaval, to persuade his body to relinquish its tension, to subside, let go, be at peace.

His eyes snapped open. In the same split second, her world blurred by then somersaulted in a burst of vertigo and friction, before colliding to a standstill with a lung-emptying slam.

She found herself flat on her back, her hands held above her head in a merciless vise, her throat pressed closed, with two hundred-plus pounds of granitelike manhood and a ton of premium male aggression pinning her to the bed.

She blinked up in shock, saw him looming over her, his face a mask of ferocity, a huge, sleek feline in killing mode, immobilizing his prey before he gouged out its neck.

He blinked, too, then again, dazed, fazed as he removed the hand that had almost choked her. "Clarissa…"

She coughed, realized he'd thought her an attacker.

How many times had he been assaulted, hurt, to develop such an ingrained, lightning-speed reflex in response to a threat?

Hot needles sprouted behind her eyes, the tears seeping from them seeming to originate from her heart.

She felt all his aggression and tension melt away just as his manhood hardened, expanded against her in acute response to feeling her beneath him, so completely accommodating.

Suddenly he let her hands go, rolled off of her and onto his back once more. This time he threw his arm over his eyes.

"*Perdonami... Dio,* Clarissa, I thought you were…were…"

She shakily dragged herself up to her elbows. "What?"

He muttered something indistinct then exhaled. "Nothing. Just what the hell are you doing here anyway, Clarissa?"

She leaned over him, feeling strain still clutching his every muscle. She needed to alleviate it, had to let him know he wasn't alone in dealing with demons that wouldn't let go. "I came looking for you. Then I…heard you. I had to come in, Ferruccio. You were having a nightmare, and I…I wanted to help." Her hands trembled as she grasped his arm, pulled it away from his eyes. "I still do."

Suspicion flared in his gaze before it dissipated and something else took over. Something that, before the past fraught minutes since she'd walked in on him, she hadn't believed him capable of feeling, let alone exhibiting. Naked emotions. Intense, permeating, sincere. She could read them all as if they were being generated inside her, were hers to experience, to revel in, to share. Relief, gratitude, need—or solace, for closeness.

He grabbed one of her hands, pressed it to his chest as his other one trembled its way to her throat. He let out a shuddering breath, as if venting the scare of his life. "*Dio Santo,* Clarissa…I could have hurt you."

She couldn't bear his guilt. She reached out with her free hand, smoothed his forehead. She cursed herself when her lips trembled and lost their grip on her smile, let it slip off. "You didn't. It was like a new kind of roller coaster. You have this flattering way of making me feel like I weigh five pounds instead of a hundred and fifty."

Those painstakingly sculpted lips of his, which had been

pressed into an austere line since he'd jerked awake, relaxed a bit, filled with a measure of his humor and sensuality. "I'm just sorry you got in the way when I was still fighting with whatever it was that invaded my dreams. For a moment there, I couldn't tell that I was awake, that it wasn't happening…anymore."

She sat up, tucked her legs beneath her, used the movement, the moment, to steady herself after that last "anymore" played havoc with her imagination, her heartbeats. "You're not talking about what you've experienced during this nightmare alone."

His eyes escaped hers. Then he seemed to decide not to evade the issue, nodded. "There've been some…bad times. They come back from time to time. I'm not sure why. It's been a very long time since I was a kid on the street fending for my life. The memories have dulled to a distant echo."

"Have they?" She didn't buy that for a second. He didn't know he was talking to an expert in childhood trauma here. "Some memories remain as clear as ever. They even take on sharper clarity with time, become augmented, having been experienced through and recorded by the impressionability and exaggeration of a child's psyche."

His eyes snapped back to hers, amazement glinting in their silver steel depths. She could almost hear him wondering where she got such insight, debating whether to broach the subject. She steeled herself for his questions, preparing evasions, but he seemed to let it go, as she'd fervently hoped, steering away from the land mine of going into her personal history, focusing on his revisited trauma. "I wasn't exactly a child when I ran away from my last foster home."

"You were before you ran away. The reasons you left must have been as…unerasable. And then, thirteen isn't that grown-up. I can't even imagine spending one day on the streets *now*, let alone when I was that age. To be that young and know I have no one to run to, no one to think of me or protect me, to even shelter me and give me a bite to eat when I'm starving…how did you do it, Ferruccio? How did you survive all that?"

His gaze wavered. His voice grew thick, impeded. "Millions of kids survive that and worse every day, all over the world."

"None have become what you've become. There's only one explanation for that. You're a miracle, Ferruccio Selvaggio."

He looked completely taken aback. Flabbergasted. He looked at her as if he thought he was still dreaming, or wading through the aftereffects of a mind-tampering drug.

He must be trying to understand what had brought on her change in attitude. To tell him that, she'd have to tell him things she never wanted to reveal. To him of all people.

Apart from the shock of hearing her admitting her admiration, her awe of him, she could see he was nowhere near back to his steely controlled self. Judging by the redness creeping beneath his razor-sharp cheekbones, he was embarrassed by her praise!

Before she could tell him it wasn't praise, just statement of fact, he shook his head. "I don't think there's any miracle involved in what I achieved. I've had as many good breaks as I've had bad ones. I haven't only been exposed to monsters who live to prey on the vulnerable just because they can, I've been gifted with finding angels who help and guide, also just because they can. I dream of them, too, even if their guest appearances don't elicit such a…dramatic response. When all is said and done, I have more to be thankful for than any man I know. And if the occasional nightmare pops up every now and then as a sort of a 'thou art mortal' reminder, it all comes with the territory."

Her lips twitched at his attempt at levity. But not with humor. With aching. She'd so recently likened him to a drunk-on-power, malicious god. His reference now to what kept him human made her realize more than ever how indescribable his ordeals had been, that he still struggled, that his imperviousness was only a perfected act.

And she realized another vital thing. The likely reason behind his reputation as a heartless womanizer who didn't let women stay the night after he'd had his pleasure. He'd wouldn't want to expose what she'd just witnessed, what he must consider a weakness, to another human being. He probably never thought of seeking solace.

Though he hadn't *chosen* to expose that Achilles' heel to her, he'd easily accepted the fact that she witnessed it and had bared more of his inner self willingly, almost eagerly.

"Grazie molto, mia bella unica."

She stared at him, truly at a loss. "For what?"

He cupped her cheek in his large, warm hand, stroked a gentle finger across the arch of her eyebrow, down her nose to the slightly parted lines of her lips. "For going up against the monsters that go bump inside my head."

The suddenness with which communion, emotional and sublime, switched to awareness, carnal and greedy, was dizzying.

Her eyes had adjusted to the subdued lights, which seemed to have been calibrated to highlight every chiseled plane of his body, every honed groove, every gleaming, silky hair accentuating each line and bulge of power. He'd already been beyond unfair when clothed. Almost naked like this...the injustice was unspeakable.

"You like?"

He'd asked her that her yesterday. Then, he'd meant the masterpiece nature and his domain combined had painted.

He was asking about another work of divine art and human perseverance here. Himself.

She swallowed, gave him the same answer. It still applied, after all. "I'm alive, am I not? I have to like."

His lips spread even as he fully did. "Then...help yourself."

Six

Clarissa didn't know where to start helping herself.

At the jut of his cheekbones, the slope of his forehead, the power of his jaw? Or should she start at the command of his brow, work down the slash of his nose to the hypnosis of that mouth that turned her inside out no matter what it said or did?

Maybe she should bypass his face for now. Take the unprecedented chance to explore his exposed perfection.

But there her choices were even more abundant. Should she start at his shoulders? Which part would she start with? That sculpted clavicle or those ripped deltoids? At his chest? At the daunting expanse of his pectorals where they tapered into the effortless strength-producing bulges of his biceps, or where they were sharply demarcated from his marble-hard six-pack? Or should she start with the raven silk hair that had the exact formation and density to emphasize each muscular mass? There was nothing but more to marvel at along every inch of the taut, polished skin encasing him in an amalgam of living, golden bronze.

And that was just the part that was exposed. The sheets hid

more. She felt almost sorry she hadn't been in any condition to stop and take stock of his below-waistline assets before.

"Let me help you help yourself," he whispered.

Still on his back, seemingly relaxed now, he reached out languidly, took both her hands, brought them to his body.

She moaned at the spike of sensation as he flattened one of her palms against his chest, over his heart, the other low on his abdomen, an inch above the sheets heaped around his hips and thighs.

"Feel that?" She knew he meant the high-voltage current it seemed his flesh was generating. She felt electrocuted and supercharged at once. She nodded. "Your touch paralyzes me with too much sensation, yet makes me feel I can leap buildings."

Just what she felt! She nodded again, more eager. His eyes were slits of passion as he started moving her hands over him, as if he were a master artist, painting an impressionist creation with broad strokes at times, with short flicks and tantalizing dabs at others. Then he brought one of her hands to his face, held it there with both of his, relinquishing the other. He showed her what to do before taking it to his mouth. He alternated between massaging its fleshy parts with nibbles to burying kisses along her palm's lines, to flicking his tongue at the junctures of her fingers, to sucking on each one as his eyes showed her he'd do all that to her everywhere else. Sensations and imaginings sent a current of arousal flowing through her, lodging in her womb.

When her hands resisted him, started to linger where they pleased, to absorb the details she'd longed to touch, he took his hands away, lay back, surrendering to her impending exploration.

Her first totally voluntary action was to cup his face, as she'd dreamed of doing for so long. As long as she could remember, it seemed. She met his eyes as she feathered her thumbs in the hollows beneath the arch of his cheekbones, glided to and fro across the sculpture of his lips, smoothing the wings of his eyebrows before caressing his heavy-with-desire lids shut.

She put her lips to each, felt him tense with every tickle of hot breath. "I did that before, to make you open your eyes, to take you away from the nightmare. Now I want you to savor this, keep your eyes closed, relax." His eyes snapped open instead, all intention of letting her explore him evaporating as he took her by the waist, by the head, tried to bring her lips to his. She resisted, burying her lips at the corner of his mouth as he'd done to her last night. "Let me, Ferruccio. I've wanted to touch you for so long."

He let her go, spread himself for her to take of him what she would. "*Si,* do everything to me, everything you want or have ever fantasized about. There are no limits, just freedom, pleasure."

She knew what her real problem was. Not that she didn't know how to help herself. But that she *couldn't* help herself.

She rubbed her aching breasts against the malleable steel of his chest, on her way to his lips. She paused to study how their chiseled planes were severe and uncompromising, how the bottom one filled into the essence of sensuality. She took it in both of hers, closing her eyes to focus on the tactile exploration, marveling at its strength and softness, its heat and moistness, that magnificent taste that was him.

His body buzzed with tension as her teeth trod her lips' path, as she nudged his lips apart with her tongue and plunged inside in search of more of that addictive taste. She felt him struggle not to grab her head and crash her mouth on his and take over. She almost wanted him to. Almost. She wanted to explore him more.

And she did. All the treasures she'd counted, she touched and tested and tasted. They were even more incredible when feasted on with all the senses.

She was running the tip of her tongue along the grooves separating his six-pack, wondering how was it possible for flesh to be so hard, so hot, to vibrate like that, when he groaned.

"Now do what you want to do most."

She obeyed, took hold of his sheet, and with heart-thudding slowness, pulled it off him. And stared.

The sheet hadn't been heaped. That height had been him. And then there was his girth, his shape.

She'd felt him last night, through their clothes, had thought he was as unique there as everywhere else. Again imagination fell way short of reality. Her mouth watered, her hands stung.

"Feel me, Clarissa," he urged, his eyes as glazed as hers. "Enjoy me, own me. Show me how good it feels to touch me, how alive it makes you feel to know you do this to me."

She was melting with need. But the enormity of what she wanted to do, what he was coaxing and commanding her to do, still overwhelmed her. She felt too inexperienced to live. Sure, she knew the mechanics. But only theoretically. She'd never touched a man. Not like this, not in any other way.

She'd been a recluse her first eighteen years, and the next four hadn't been much better as she poured all her focus and energy into her studies and sports. She'd rebuffed approaches, not only because they targeted her to exploit her status, to "score with a princess," but because she hadn't been interested in anyone.

Then she met *him*. And she knew. It was him or no one. And since she'd believed it would never be him, she believed she'd never know a man's touch. Now she knew it—*his* touch. Now she could touch and see and feel and exult—in him. Only him.

Her hand tried to close around him, couldn't. She swallowed as he throbbed in her grasp, as her skin absorbed the fusion of softness and hardness, the heat coursing in his shaft. He echoed her moan with a long groan as she stroked him. She watched pleasure slash across his hewn face, his muscled hips flexing as he thrust to her rhythm and watched her with mounting hunger. She worshipped him, brought her face down to his power and scent, all him, all male. She couldn't help herself again.

She flicked her tongue across his erection's crown, almost passed out at feeling the slick satin of his flesh against her tongue, his tangy taste against her taste buds. She inhaled deep to draw oxygen to her brain and only drew his scent into her lungs. With a cry of urgency, she opened her mouth to take in all she could of him.

His hand twisted in her hair, stopped her.

She whimpered. "I want to taste your pleasure."

"You will. As I will taste yours, over and over. But I want our first pleasure together to be flesh in flesh."

She wanted that, too. She was dying for that. But then, she was dying for everything. All at once. But he wanted that first. She was dying to give him everything he wanted.

She felt clumsy after the abandon of feasting on him, didn't know what to do now. Her gaze wavered to his face as he sat up.

His eyes burned a path down her short-sleeved, form-fitting top and its matching stretch pants. "Not a skirt suit, and yet another outfit that will forever feature in my most erotic fantasies. I want it off you. Now, Clarissa."

Without a word or thought, thankful for the instruction, she crossed her hands at the hem of her top and pulled it over her head. She wanted it off, too. Couldn't bear the friction of cloth on her burning skin, the imprisonment of her swollen flesh.

He growled something predatory at the sight of her breasts, fuller with arousal in the confines of her bra, deepening her cleavage. She fell back on the bed with the blow of arousal that slammed into her at the sound, the intention behind it.

He rose to his knees above her. "More, Clarissa. Show me the rest of you. Bare yourself fully to me. Drive me totally crazy."

Her hands felt unmatched as she struggled with the button and zip of her pants. She shuddered all over as she tried to wriggle out of them. He watched her writhe before him, the ferocity in his eyes mounting. Then he exploded to his feet on top of the bed, bent and picked up her legs, raised her by them until only her shoulders and head touched the bed. He stared down at her, their harsh pants of stimulation filling the air.

She knew how she must look to him, held in his power upside down like that, half-fainting, wanting and inviting anything he'd do to her, lying in a pool of her hair, her breasts almost spilling from her bra under the pull of gravity, her stretch pants bunched midway down her thighs, her light purple panties stained by the darkness of her desire for him, the legs he held trying as hard as they could to pull him down, bring him between them.

Then in one swipe, like a magician, he had her stretch pants off.

He lowered her legs to the bed, stood above her, eating her alive with his eyes before he came down, prowled on all fours over her, until his powerful limbs became a prison of muscle and maleness all around her. "*Mia bella unica.* You are the miracle. And you were right. I'm very good at hiding my insanity. For six years, I've been insane." His hands dipped beneath her and she arched up, helping him as he undid her bra. He peeled it off and her swollen breasts fell into his palms. She cried out as he pressed them together, mitigating the ache, increasing the need. He bent and showed her there was more suffering, more pleasure. Between long, hard pulls on her nipples, he swirled them with his tongue, grazed them with his teeth, blew the stimulation of his confessions on them. "You made me lose my mind with a look, a word. And that was before I touched you. Last night, early this morning, every gasp and moan, your pleasure and desire, whether I see them or feel them or imagine them, make me go mad. You were born to drive me to distraction."

"Ferruccio, please..." This time she knew what she was begging for. "Don't wait...I can't...I can't..."

His hands clamped her buttocks, squeezed and fondled, before he rid them of that last barrier in another magical move. "There will be no more waiting. Never again, do you hear?"

"Yes, yes...please." Her quaking thighs opened for him, unashamedly offering, hurrying, begging.

He took his erection in his hand, but instead of driving into her, filling the emptiness gnawing at her, he glided the scorching head, flowing with his own arousal, through the engorged lips of her sex until he reached her slit. Her flesh fluttered around what it could reach of his hardness, as if trying to grab onto him, drag him inside her.

"Do you see how wet and hot and ready for me you are?" He glided up, nudged her most sensitive knot of flesh. She rose off the bed with a shrill cry of surprise and ecstasy. "When you were touching yourself for me, what were you imagining, Clarissa? Was it my fingers fondling you, my tongue licking you…or this?"

He glided down then up again, circled her swollen knot until she writhed, everything in the world, all reason and meaning focusing where his flesh tormented hers.

She keened her confession. "This…I saw you, felt you doing this…I was dying for you to do it for real. But this is a thousand times better…I never knew…*anything*…could feel this good."

"Neither did I. And it'll only get better." He slid down a second before she came apart, then he thrust into her slit in compulsive strokes, shallow, fast, almost uncoordinated, his face driven.

Even as coherence seeped out of her, she realized he wasn't in control of himself. His actions weren't premeditated. He was as lost as she. And she knew something else. No one else had ever seen his vulnerability, provoked his uncontrollable need. Only her.

The conviction spread through her like a rush of lifesaving water after she'd been parched and withering.

She hooked her legs around him, tried to pull him, bring him inside her. She knew it would hurt. She wanted it to. She wanted him to brand her this first time.

Then he did. He lunged, tearing through her barrier, then plunging past into the depths that yielded for him, feeling like a sword just out of the fire. She screamed, writhed with the pain, with its excruciating pleasure, with the carnality, the completion of Ferruccio dominating her and surrendering to her captivation.

"*Dio, Dio santo*…so tight, so hot. Clarissa, *amore*…you're burning me." Her face was clenched in what looked like suffering as he withdrew then plunged deeper, again, and again, forging farther inside her, feeling as if he'd never bottom out. "Burn me, *cuore mio,* consume me as I invade you, take all of me, all the way inside you, all the way to the heart of you."

He did feel he was all the way inside her. For a moment she thought he'd reached her heart for real. And he had—the heart of her femininity, her womb. That intimate nudge was beyond anything she'd dreamed of. Beyond endurance. Just the concept of it, the reality! All her life, everything she'd ever felt for him, every spark of sensation gathered into one pinpoint of absolute being, of experiencing everything at once. Then it exploded.

She convulsed, shattered, then reformed for the next wave. She heard screams accompanying the rending ecstasy razing through her. Then she heard his roar, felt him stiffen in her clutching arms, ramming her deeper than ever before, breaching her completely as jet after jet of warmth flooded her. His release. His seed, filling her. Her first intimacy, her only man, taking his pleasure inside her as he gave her more than pleasure.

She shook, writhed, wept. Then… Nothing.

Ferruccio felt Clarissa slump beneath him, her satin limbs sliding off him like the shedded petals of a rose.

Panic mushroomed in his chest as he took his weight off her inert body on shaking arms. He groaned as he withdrew from the depths that still clutched him, a prisoner to her possession.

He frantically examined her. Her face, streaked in tears, her lips, shining and plum red, parted…and gusting tranquil breaths.

He collapsed beside her. *Dio*…for a moment there he'd thought…

He shook his head in self-deprecation. Had he started to believe his own reputation as a lady-killer?

He rose again and looked down at her, all of her, all the treasures he hadn't been in any condition to slow down and savor, when his first exposure to them had driven him into a frenzy.

Which wasn't an excuse for pouncing on her like he had.

For six years he'd promised himself that the first time he got her in his bed, he'd pamper and service her until he had her weeping with satisfaction before taking his.

He'd achieved that, had her in such acute pleasure, she'd wept. In an agony of release she came so hard that she fainted. But that wasn't the refined, protracted seduction he'd planned on. He'd lost control.

He'd never before come within miles of losing control.

But he'd touched her, and he'd become a mindless predator bound on branding his mark on his mate.

And how he had. He was shaken at the enormity of the experience. Branding her as his had been the first surrender of his life, his first real and total pleasure. But she'd branded him as hers, too. As he'd known she would when he'd first seen her and those intense feelings of possession, of belonging, had come over him. Before her rejection had swathed his feelings in harshness of bitterness, resentment and anger…

He ran a hand heavy with possession over her. His. At last.

He gathered her cooling body to him, took her into his still shaking arms…and froze. Beneath her. A tiny pool of blood.

Panic surged again. It subsided within a moment. The location and amount of the blood said it all; he'd been her first.

The discovery shook him. Elated him. Made him want to pound his chest and do backflips. She *had* been his all along.

But…if she had been, why had she put him—and herself—through all this? Why had it taken him going all caveman on her to make her give them this at last?

He looked down at the face etched by satiation, transformed by the experience. The image of all his dreams and fantasies, and far beyond both. And his rage crept back.

Why was he even wondering? He'd always known why.

He'd always felt her answering craving, felt her holding it on a tight leash, evading him so she wouldn't succumb to the temptation. Because it had been abhorrent to her. *He* had been. She might have decided to give in to her hunger now, since he'd made it in her best interest to do so.

He'd told her to persuade him, but she'd come here not bent on persuasion but on conquering. And when she'd gone up in flames in his arms, she *had* conquered him. If she could do this to him without experience, he failed to imagine what kind of hold she'd have on him when she gained sexual confidence. Now that he'd tasted her, he was already addicted. He had to have more—all of her.

Disappointment twisted inside him, damaging things he hadn't known existed there. Hope, need, dependency. All the things she'd unearthed in him since he'd first seen her, things she brought into the open when she'd seen him without his shields. She'd offered him a haven of her very self, given him a purity he'd never experienced, of appreciation, of empathy and eagerness to defuse his turmoil, to defend him against the shadows of his past.

And all along she'd remained the woman who despised him in her heart. There was no other explanation for the past years or her recent resistance. He should stop fooling himself, stop looking for excuses to exonerate her.

Not that that made any difference now. Now, she was his. And she'd remain his. As he'd remain hers.

Not that he was handing her power over him. Ever. He was getting what he wanted from her, and giving back only what would keep her in his power, in every way.

A wisp of gossamer slid down her face, her neck, her breast, the soothing contentment of it flowed until it suddenly turned into an electric current that zapped to her head, forked to her toes, turned to another pulse of heavy need between her legs.

Her eyes snapped open. He filled her vision in the now candlelit darkness.

Ferruccio. The man she'd been running from for what felt like her whole life. Spread out on his side beside her, propped on one elbow, running his hands in appreciation up and down the body he'd possessed, awakened, ravaged, satisfied, all to the point that she'd lost consciousness for the first time in her life.

This, him, was what she'd waited for for six years. And for all her life before she'd ever seen him, when she must have known on some level that he existed. Finding him had been like finding the answer to the incompleteness she'd suffered. Losing him, the hope and endless possibilities of him, had been a loss she dedicated herself to recovering from, to living with.

She'd been deluded. She'd thought what he made her feel yesterday and this morning was all she could feel. Now she knew what he could do to her every time his hands glided over her, his lips and teeth owned her, his potency filled and rode her. She knew the meaning of yearning.

It went far beyond the physical. After what they'd shared before they made love, then the way he let her have him before he had her, it spanned everything she was capable of feeling.

She'd long escaped admitting it. She could run no more.

She loved him.

How she loved him. With everything in her.

And it changed nothing. She was just a convenience for him.

Or was she? The things he'd said, the way he'd treated her, taken her…could he possibly feel more for her than she believed?

"That was some persuasion." Her heart lurched at the tone of his voice. The passion and sincerity were gone. He rose above her, and his eyes were filled with lust untouched by anything softer or higher. "But I already feel the need to be persuaded some more. I'll need constant persuasion from now on."

She plummeted from heaven to crash into cold reality. His.

Here was her answer. She was another victory. A strategic one, guaranteed to put so many pieces of his plan into place.

He found her secrets, her triggers, disintegrating her body into pleasure even as he smashed her heart into smaller pieces. And she did the only thing she could to ward off the pain. She matched his nonchalance, his coldness.

"I assume you're satisfied with my test drive? You must be extra pleased to find me in brand-new condition."

He gave a cruel chuckle. "You have no idea. Let me demonstrate the level of my pleasure on your own made-for-pleasure body."

He rose from the bed and carried her to his bathroom, where he'd prepared a bubbling bath. He took her into the soothing waters, bathed her and healed her. His hands glided over her, possessing her, possessing the ability to dissolve her shackles, release her potential. He made her feel both vulnerable and all-powerful. Savored and devoured. He had her writhing, pleading. He made her watch his hand delve between her thighs. His fingers knew just where and how hard or gentle or fast to touch, plunging and withdrawing, stroking, stoking until he had her heaving with a screeching orgasm.

His mouth milked hers for each last shriek as his fingers changed rhythm, desensitizing her, infusing her with renewed desperation. He growled satisfaction at her resurrected hunger, as he raised her onto the marble platform by the tub, laid her there on her back, her legs parted and bent at its edge. He tormented his way down her heaving body, took her legs over his shoulders, came to lie where it all converged. "Open for me, *amore.* I'm hungry."

Incoherent under the pressure mushrooming in her loins, she opened wide for him. Legs and heart and abandon.

He bent to her quivering flesh, swept her in a long lick that knocked her internal lights out before he fused his tongue and teeth there and suckled and flicked until she thought something inside her was charring, until her body gushed molten agony, trembled with detonation after detonation of satisfaction. He sucked every spasm out of her in a tongue-thrusting kiss that went on until he again had her climbing, clawing, crazed. Ready for him again.

Her eyes clung to his as he lifted her from the platform where she lay in a pool of sweat, bathwater and condensed steam, dried her, carried her back to the bedroom and laid her down on the bed. Candlelight and moonlight cast flickering gold and steady silver over his rugged planes as he came over her, intersecting at arcane shadows. He bore down on her, opened her around his hips, raised hers and held them in one hand, the other supporting him as he rose halfway on both knees. Then he plunged.

He knew. Knew that she was suffocating to have his flesh in hers, the razing friction, the beyond-her-limits expansion. And he gave it all to her. Impaled her to her womb, her gut, her heart.

He slammed into her and she screamed for more. Then the tidal wave was cresting again. She pleaded his name, begging him to join her in oblivion. He did, in jets of completion, roars of surrender.

He came down beside her, tenderness back in his eyes, his hands, the coldness burned away in the inferno of what they'd shared.

And through the night, though he wouldn't take her again, said he shouldn't have taken her again so soon, he pleasured her in so many ways. And in every touch, every word, he confessed his pleasure, his inability to get enough. As did she.

Midday sun poured through the open windows when she next woke up. She was alone in bed.

She jerked up, looking for Ferruccio.

He found him standing on the other side of the bed, fully dressed, hands in pockets, looking down at her broodingly.

Her heart sank. In this insanity-inducing game of hot and cold that he played, were they back to cold?

His eyes said they were. Then his words completed the frost. "Now that your 'test drive' has proved so mutually and mind-blowingly pleasurable, I'm moving to the next logical step. Marriage."

Seven

Clarissa rose cautiously.

The soreness between her legs forced the carefulness. That, plus feeling as if she'd frozen and might shatter at any sudden move. She scooped up her clothes without looking at him, went to the bathroom.

She remained there for an hour, trying to regain some composure.

She came out to find him at the far end of the room, at his reading table. She walked over to him, running the words she'd decided to say through her head one more time.

She stopped before him, recited them. "I want to thank you for the tremendous initiation, but now I demand that you keep up your end of the deal, become crown prince and leave me alone."

Ferruccio gave her a bored smile. "This is getting old. When will you think before you talk? You now, more than ever, have no option but to fall in with my plans. I have no option but to marry you, either. That you were in 'brand-new-condition' is exactly why neither of us has another option."

"Taking my virginity doesn't mean we have to get married."

"Taking *you* twice, without protection, does," he retorted. "You could already be pregnant."

Everything stilled as the blow registered. A quick calculation told her he could be right. She felt she was falling into an abyss. "Even if I am, it isn't your responsibility. I'm way over the age of consent, and I consented to everything that happened. If I'm pregnant, I'll handle it on my own."

His benign boredom evaporated in a tide of aggression as he rose, neared her. "*Handle* it? As in an abortion? Or maybe have the baby then put it up for adoption?"

His most sensitive issue.

How dared he think her capable of either course of action!

"If I'm pregnant," she seethed. "I'll have the baby and love it for the rest of my life. You needn't concern yourself."

His scowl was spectacular. "You know nothing about me, do you? No child of mine is growing up a bastard."

"That's an antiquated view!" she cried out. "Millions of single moms raise children alone."

His lips curled. "Save your opinion about the advantages of single motherhood until you've been one. And then you shouldn't speak for your child. Would you, who had the benefit of two loving parents, deprive your child of the same security? Would you, a princess in a conservative kingdom steeped in family values, brave being an unmarried mother? Or would you leave Castaldini to be one, all so that you can have the last word? So you won't have to submit to me? So you can spite me?"

She flinched as his voice rose on the last words, his sudden move bringing her arm up in an instinctive blocking gesture.

She lowered it at once, praying he hadn't noticed her action.

But he noticed everything.

He looked at her as if *she* had dealt *him* a crippling blow.

He at last rasped, "*Dio santo,* you thought…you thought I was going to…*hit* you?" She looked determinedly away. "Clarissa! Look at me. Did you think I would? Don't you know that I'd sooner cut off both my arms than lay a hand on you in anything but passion?"

"Anger is a passion," she mumbled.

"No, anger is a weakness," he snapped. "Venting it in physical abuse is a *crime.* I never give in to the first, will never be guilty of the second. But I'm certain someone's hit you before. Who was it? I demand to know who the sick wretch is."

She escaped his seeking hands. "Leave me alone, Ferruccio."

He caught her back. "I will never leave you alone. And you will tell me who scarred you to the point that you cringed at my sudden move, expecting a blow. This hasn't happened once before, it has happened repeatedly. You've come to expect violence to be the only way someone would express their displeasure."

"Let me go, damn you."

"I won't let you go until you tell me who did this to you."

"So you're physically restraining me to make me bow to your will? And you think you're any better than the person who hit me? Both of you use physical force to vent your frustrations and impose your warped will."

He let her go abruptly, and she felt as if she'd lost all anchors. His grip hadn't even been uncomfortable. It had been possessive but not coercive, filled with a power that had told her it would be used on her behalf, would never be turned against her.

"Fine, don't tell me," he gritted. "It's easy for me to figure out who it is. You haven't had any relationships with men, so it couldn't have been a stranger. It has to be a family member. And it could only be one. Your father."

"No."

"Yes. Who else could get away with abusing you? Your brothers wouldn't have. I *know* them. I'm going to take him apart."

"Ferruccio, stop it. You're not coming near him."

"Don't worry, I won't give him a taste of his own medicine,

even if compared to me he's as helpless as the child you were when he abused you. I can deliver hits that will hurt far more than kicks and blows. I will dethrone that twisted bastard and exile him. He'll never have the privilege of coming near you again!"

"You're wrong, he…didn't…" She felt she'd faint again.

"Don't defend him, Clarissa, or my punishment of him will only be harsher, last far longer."

"You just want to punish him, but not for me, for yourself."

He went still. "What do you mean by that?"

"You think he's the reason you remained unacknowledged by your family, and you're using me as an excuse to hurt him as you imagine he's hurt you."

He cracked a harsh laugh. "I couldn't care less about the acknowledgement of my so-called family. The two D'Agostinos who've become a part of my life haven't done so through the ties of blood—which I think are grossly overrated—but through mutual respect, through clicking on fundamental levels, through being able to like and count on one another. As for the rest of the extensive D'Agostino clan, I care nothing for their opinion of me, or their existence in this world one way or another. In fact, I think if those people had had any presence in my life, they would have only hindered me. I believe that by hiding me from them, your father has actually protected me from their interference and negative influences. So not having the 'acknowledgement of my family' certainly won't be why I'll punish him. I'll punish him for you, and only for you."

She grabbed his arm, shook him. "You won't come near him, do you hear? Or…or you'll never come near me again!"

He bared his teeth. "He abused you—"

"He *didn't!* He *protected* me!"

"From *whom?* Who could have had such access to you, a princess, that your father, the king, had to protect you from them?"

And she wailed, "*It was my mother.*"

This shocked him so much she felt his whole body stiffen

as if against a brutal blow, saw his face seize with horror and confusion. "How? *Dio*…why?"

She shook her head dejectedly. "Just leave it be, Ferruccio."

"You didn't 'leave it be' when you woke me from my nightmare. You wanted to know, to help. You think I can do anything less?"

"As you said, it's in the past. It has been for twenty years."

"And it's clearer than ever in your memory. Having been 'experienced through the impressionability and exaggeration of a child's psyche.'"

She grimaced. "You have total recall, don't you?"

His lips compressed. "You should know by now that I can't be distracted when I'm bent on something. *Tell* me."

"You didn't really tell me anything. Why should I tell you?"

"I'll tell you everything down to the last detail you can possibly stomach. All you have to do is ask. Now start talking."

She knew he'd get it out of her one way or another. She gave in, shrugged. "She was having marital troubles with my father…"

"And she took it out on you?"

"She had a psychiatric disorder, I guess."

"You guess? She wasn't diagnosed? Treated?"

"She never admitted there was anything wrong with her. Lack of insight supports the opinion that she was deeply disturbed. You see, my mother was very beautiful and she'd been pursued since she was a teenager. Her father, a very rich and influential man, believed all her pursuers were fortune hunters. He drove them away then turned on her to 'discipline' her. Especially when she got attached to one of them for a while."

"He hit her when she was old enough to get married?"

"Do you want me to talk, or do you want to play commentator and analyst?" He raised an eyebrow, made a mock-contrite gesture for her to go on. "My grandfather then arranged her marriage to my father, a self-made billionaire and the new king of Castaldini, someone he thought worthy of his only heiress. Everything went like a fairy tale, and they had two male heirs to their lineage and combined fortunes, if not to the crown. But in truth, things went from bad to worse between her and my father. It seems they conceived me during one of their last attempts at being a couple. An attempt that failed. After I was born, they were unofficially separated and my mother focused on me to a pathological level."

"She wouldn't let you out in the sun, to play in the sea like all children should. She told you it was for your own good when she was using you to anesthetize her pain. She made you her life's project so she could have an excuse to suffocate you, used her innocent little girl as an antidote to her failure to earn the dependence of someone who had a choice. And when it didn't stop her pangs, she punished you for it."

She gave a mocking sigh. "Okay, I'm shutting up now. You're ready to write a book analyzing my mother's character, motivations and every last action."

"I became who I am by reading people accurately from a single word or action."

He was so outrageously sure of himself. And so right to be. She sighed again. "Yeah. You're so good, sometimes I think you read minds. So…now you know. How about we drop this?"

"And continue the other eagerly anticipated subject we were discussing before we diverged into that delightful revelation, you mean? All in due course. You haven't finished this story. Tell me how this ended, your father's role in this mess. Where was he when your mother was suffocating you and systematically abusing you?"

"Listen, don't try to swing this back into my father's corner. I won't let you. He was the king and he had a job to do, a very complex job as you'll discover, if it becomes yours one day. My mother kept me in her apartments, and he had no reason to think anything was wrong. Apart from dogging my every step and controlling my every breath until I was about five, she was sort of okay. But I admit, I was a handful. Hyperactive and rebellious, never responding until she yelled at me or shook me, never obeying any order until threatened and punished."

"Good for you."

She hugged herself. "Not really. I think I drove her over the edge."

"She told you that, didn't she?" he snarled.

"When she started hitting me for real? Yeah, she said I made her do it, being so naughty."

"Every abuser's excuse. That their victim made them do it."

"I guess so. She…she also kept saying she hated me for being so like my father, that she hated him because he stopped loving her." She paused to gulp a breath and to brace herself against the terrible sound his teeth made gritting against each other. "Then it was over, just like that. A few days after my eighth birthday, Durante walked in unannounced and found her…found her…"

"Hitting you. How did she hit you, Clarissa?"

"How do people hit? The usual way."

"I've hit many people in my life. Bullies bigger than me or equals who attacked me first. But since I hit to end an aggression, I hit hard, go for the face. She didn't touch your face, did she? That was how she got away with it, leaving no marks on you. She covered you from head to toe in clothes and said you sunburn easily when she was covering the bruises she inflicted on you. She wasn't so crazy after all, was she, if she gave covering her crime that much care and premeditation?" Clarissa could no longer find air to breathe. He'd sucked it all out of her world with his insight, the way he'd framed what she'd always shied away from seeing, realizing. "How was she hitting you when Durante walked in?"

"She—she was kicking me. In the stomach."

There was that terrible grinding sound again, accompanied by the marrow-chilling purr of an enraged lion. "Did he hit her?"

"Would you have hit your mother in the same situation?"

He bared his teeth. "*Maledizione, si…*hell, yes."

"Well, Durante isn't you. He isn't used to violence or so quick to use his fists. And he'd had years with her when she was whole, when he adored her. He'd been torn over her deterioration for a long time, and he was so shocked to witness what he did. He had believed that I was her world, all that she lived for anymore. He restrained her, took her kicks and spitting and ranting that she hated him, too, for being so like our father. Then he took me away, gave me to Antonia, then went to our father and demanded that I be removed from my mother's apartments and care, forever. And I was. My father took me to his apartments and I've been safe ever since."

"What happened to your mother?"

"She seemed to…give up. On everything."

"Only abusing you gave her the will to go on, eh?"

"Please, Ferruccio. She's still my mother."

"She forfeited her right to be your mother the first time she hit you to vent her self-absorbed anger and petty frustrations."

She tried to huff a laugh. It came out a distressed rasp. "If that was universally applied, no one would have mothers or fathers anymore."

His scowl deepened. "You know what I mean. She injured you, repeatedly, systematically, got more vicious as time went by. She could have killed you."

"I don't think it would have gone that far. And after a few years, I—I became sort of her keeper, until I went to college. She wasn't the same woman who abused me anymore…and I—I loved her."

"How could you love someone who scarred you like that?"

She cast her filled eyes downward. "You wouldn't understand."

"Because I didn't have a loving mother who made all my nightmares come true, you mean? Now I'm really thankful I didn't. At least my nightmares were inflicted by strangers."

"I know it's inexplicable, the unbreakable bond a child forms with the first one who holds and cares for her. And she *did* care for me, in her way. There were good times, like you said, before and after the abusive period. And on the whole, I am far luckier than most women I know, too. I have amazing brothers, I'm healthy, I achieve good things, I live in a fairy-tale palace and I'm the daughter of the best king and father in the world. I bet any woman on earth would switch places with me in a second."

He caught his lip in vicious, white teeth, as if holding back something even he thought he shouldn't say. Then he said, "What I don't get is, after they found out your mother had been abusing you, how did they still turn you over to that Antonia battle-axe?"

A laugh burst out of her. His lips thinned. He thought she was going to make light of it, wasn't allowing it. "Sorry. It's just I always mentally, and very fondly, refer to her as a battleship! And here you are, coming up with something very close. But let me tell you, between my father's gentleness, Durante's protectiveness, Paolo's companionship and Antonia's discipline—which was as invaluable as her name proclaims her to be, and which was never in any way excessive and nothing but constructive—they probably saved my sanity. I think I turned out okay."

"As I said before, you turned out far beyond okay."

"Yeah, yeah, a merciless, shameless siren."

"As accurate an assessment as I ever made. One I can't be more thankful for. In case you're thinking of contesting my verdict, remember what you did to me all through the night. When you were fresh out of your box, too." He tugged on her, plastered her against him, showing her what she was doing to him now. "Which brings us back to our original discussion. Say yes, Clarissa."

How could she? And how could she tell him that the discussion they'd just had was why she was resisting?

She'd been running scared because she knew she'd fall for him all the way to no return. She'd been right. She now felt him mixed with her very blood and breath. He was more than she ever thought could be found in one man.

But he was incapable of intimacy. He had friends, allies, employees who worshipped the ground he walked on, but so did her father. Her father loved his children, his people, but hadn't been able to love the woman who'd literally lost her mind over him. Her mother had accused him of loving another, but Clarissa believed she'd been looking for reasons that he hadn't been able to love *her.* Her father and Ferruccio both seemed to have a glitch in their makeup. They were great men, but when it came to women it seemed they were incapable of loving one, or really loving any.

And just as her father was into leading, inspiring, Ferruccio was into vanquishing, acquiring. Sure, he made his acquisitions eternally grateful to be his. As he'd made her. But could she live with it, if that was all he could give her?

He was choosing her, using the same cerebral premeditation with which her father had chosen her mother. But it was even worse in their situation. Her mother didn't start out loving her father, and she was almost certain her father didn't set out to enslave her mother physically, like Ferruccio was doing to her.

Which meant it would be even worse for her.

But he was right, as he invariably was. If she was pregnant, her own life and emotions had to give way to her baby's. Just like her mother again. Not that she was like her mother in that she would follow the same path of psychological degeneration. Even if her heart was destroyed, she'd never take it out on her child. She'd do all she could to be the best mother she could be.

But she still had to try one final attempt to save herself.

She pushed out of his arms. "If I become pregnant, I'll marry you. If not, you become crown prince without me in the equation."

Would he *ever* learn?

Ferruccio wrestled with the tsunami of fury and offense that threatened to burst his arteries.

She made marrying him sound like an amputation, a drastic

measure to be resorted to only if all efforts to save the limb—in this case her life, from his infection—failed.

He struggled to summon the unfathomable facade that had been one of his major weapons as he considered her conditions.

If he agreed to them, she'd either end up married to him for the baby, or he'd find himself king of Castaldini without her by his side. Neither situation was acceptable.

So he countered her bargain. "We'll marry, *now.* I will wait until we're married to take you again. Give you time to heal." He gave her a taunting smile. "And to…miss me so much the wedding night will make last night pale into nothing." He saw her nipples jut against her top, conquer the thickness of both bra and top, knew her body was readying itself for his, needing him to ride it, pound it, satisfy it. But he wouldn't take her again until she begged. Again. And he would make her reach the begging point. "If you wish, I'll use protection, or you can protect yourself. If you are already pregnant, our immediate marriage will prevent speculation about the timing of our baby's conception. If you aren't, and in say, six months' time, we consider marriage between us not a viable endeavor, I'll let you leave my bed and we'll quietly separate. We can go on living in the palace without ever crossing each other's path. And if, one day, either of us wants an end to the marriage, to marry another perhaps, we'll work out something civil."

As she gaped at him, he congratulated himself for making it sound as if he wasn't desperate for her to say yes, as if she had a way out, if she wanted it, along the road, so she wouldn't panic and still say no.

But he would *make* her say yes. And keep on saying it. Forever.

This was his life's main objective now.

And he always got what he set his mind on.

Eight

"So now we know the exact time the world will come to an end."

Clarissa winced. Her friend's taunt, combined with looking at Ferruccio across the ballroom, made her feel as if she was wading in déjà vu.

Which was a misleading sensation. Apart from the same setting and faces, this occasion was poles apart from that first one.

Then, he'd been a stranger to her father's court. Now he resided over what would be his own.

Another major difference was that she'd escaped him then. Now she found no escape from his logic. Or her own weakness, which kept whispering that in six-months' time, she could become more than his convenient bride. With that hope prodding her and her love igniting its flame into an inferno, she'd capitulated.

The moment she had, yesterday, he'd taken her back to meet with her father and the Council to announce his acceptance and their decision to get married. Immediately.

They'd been in the general assembly chamber, and Ferruccio had just estimated that, to prepare the wedding befitting his princess and future queen, he needed six days. She'd been wondering if he was playing up the god connection when her father had dropped his biggest bomb yet. He was abdicating.

She vaguely remembered hearing him say he was no use as king anymore, that he wanted Ferruccio to have the full range of authority to turn around Castaldini's situation right away, that he wanted Ferruccio to be crowned king during his lifetime, *and* on the same day he married Clarissa.

"So, do you think five days is enough time for us all to make peace with each other, to say good-bye to this life and prepare for the next? Can't you convince your groom-to-be to give us more time? I'd say this mean feat needs at least a couple of weeks."

Clarissa rounded on her friend. "Oh, Luci, shut up."

Luci's eyes gleamed unrepentantly. "You know the price of my silence. Spill."

"What's to spill? You know everything."

Luci narrowed her eyes. "I was born a good bit before yesterday, you know. You're telling me, or I'm walking up to your godly hunk and asking him for his version of the developments. I bet he'd be willing to share…" She stopped, groaned. "I didn't mean it *that* way." Clarissa's lips twisted. Luci's embarrassment evaporated. "But you know that. So?"

Clarissa shrugged. "He asked me to marry him, and I agreed."

"Okay, our king, in five days' time, seems about to have an opening in the queue waiting to suck up to him. I'm running to take that spot in three…two…"

Clarissa rolled her eyes. "Okay, okay. What do you want to know?"

"You slept with him, didn't you?" Clarissa gaped at her friend. She knew Luci was straightforward, but she still hadn't imagined that would be her first question out of the gate. "Don't answer that. I know you did. You're radiating it."

Clarissa held her hand up, turned it back and forth. "I am?"

Luci snickered. "Cute. And you are. And he is, too. Remember that first night when you turned to look at him across the ballroom? It was as if you generated a field of attraction between you. That was why I was so stunned when he approached me and Stella, and then when you tried to pretend he didn't exist from then on. It was weirder when I sensed that he was always on your mind."

"Everyone's a psychic nowadays."

"Not me." Clarissa closed her eyes at the sound of the new voice. Antonia. Just what she needed. To be sandwiched between the two and only busybodies in her life, now of all times. "I certainly didn't see this coming. Not this fast, anyway. When I told you to go snatch him up, you took it to heart, didn't you, *ragazza impertinenta?*"

"She's not only a naughty girl," Luci complained. "She's downright wicked. She won't tell me details!"

Clarissa wondered if the earth had ever truly swallowed anyone. Now would be a good time. She was so ready to disappear.

Antonia looked at Clarissa shrewdly, her fighter jet–fast mind working it out. "*Si,* do tell us details. You were gone for a night and you returned with him on your arm, in an obscene hurry to get married and unable to tear his eyes off you. It must have been one hell of a night, to land you a man like Ferruccio Selvaggio."

Clarissa choked on shock. "And to think I lived all these years thinking you were a conservative pain, *bambinàia.*"

"Me? Conservative? By the time I was your age I'd had three lovers, and I've since had two husbands, God rest their souls."

"Donna Antonia conservative? She's a regular black widow!"

Antonia and Luci had overlapped. They looked at each other, Luci in impish challenge, Antonia in I'll-get-you-later threat.

Then Antonia sighed. "You were every nanny's dream charge as you grew up, one guaranteed to never get herself in trouble. But then you passed the age of consent...."

"About a century ago!" Luci put it.

Antonia glared at her, yet nodded. "What she said. And it got really old, this puritanical existence you led. I'd look at you and seethe with the waste of all that vital womanhood, especially with the epitome of manhood hanging around, courting you and getting rebuffed for his trouble. Now I'm wondering if you've just been devilishly clever all along."

"You mean, have I been sexually active and pulling the wool over your eyes?" Antonia's eyes wavered in surprise. "Hey, you can say intrusive stuff, and I can't say things like that?"

Antonia glowered. "If you were, and it wasn't with him, then you were a colossal fool."

"Then you'll be happy to know I wasn't a fool, colossal or otherwise, with him or with anyone else."

Luci poked her in the chest. "Till two days ago. I'm sure of it. You looked like another person then. Now you've…"

"Turned into some sort of radiator." Clarissa smirked at Antonia's confusion. "Previous bit of conversation before you barged in, *bambinàia*."

Antonia gave Luci a sideways glance. "And you, too, are a colossal fool, *ragazza delinquente,* that you haven't found yourself a man till now. And I mean a permanent one."

"Who knew my abstinence method would work better in the end?" Clarissa poked her friend back, taunting *her* for a change.

Luci poked back. "Hey. All I had were a couple of nonstarters. But I have to face it—not every woman is going to find herself a Ferruccio. Or a Durante. Or a Leandro. Or even a finger's worth of them. You're just plain lucky." Luci's eyes glowed with mischief, assuring Clarissa there wasn't the least tinge of envy in her friend's heart. "So…just *how* lucky were you? On a scale from one to a hundred?"

Clarissa's gaze panned to where Ferruccio stood. His eyes clung to her even as he talked to Castaldini's ambassador to France and his whole family. She turned to the two looking expectantly at her, let out a ragged exhalation. "A billion."

Both women gaped. Then Antonia burst out guffawing, "I knew it!" while Luci fanned herself furiously.

Suddenly Luci exclaimed, *"Citi che il gatto e lui viene salando."*

Clarissa had felt Ferruccio's decision to seek her out before she realized what Luci meant. The Castaldinian proverb "mention the tomcat and he comes bounding."

Every cell went into hyperdrive at his approach. She saw the other two women's faces light up in admiration, in anticipation of what they'd witness. The sound level in the buzzing ballroom dropped. It seemed everyone wanted to watch the interaction between their impending king and queen, now that the formal part of the evening was over.

Then he was behind her. She held her breath. What would he do?

The last thing she expected him to, of course.

He wrapped her in his arms, buried his scalding lips into her neck in open-mouthed kisses up to her ear. *"Ti manco?"*

Miss him? She'd spent last night tossing in her bed as if she were in the clutches of an unremitting fever. As she had been. And she'd bet he'd known that would be her condition. She considered her answer.

Nonchalant pretense? *Not really.* Sullen challenge? *Why should I?* Truthful fury? *You know I did, damn you into infinity!*

Then she decided her best answer.

She turned around in his arms, snaked hers around his neck, failed to bury her fingers in the too-short, thick silk at his nape, dragged his head down and brought his lips to hers.

After a second of stiffening surprise, his growl filled her as he his tongue did, took her over, thrust deep.

Even as she disintegrated in the pleasure of him again, the relief and freedom of letting what she felt show, a burst of noise impinged on her fogged awareness. She thought she heard claps and hoots among the uproar.

When Ferruccio let her up for air, looking down at her as if he'd haul her over his shoulder and storm off to his bed—or drag her down to the floor—she dazedly turned to her companions.

Antonia had joined Luci in fanning herself as she exclaimed, "Now I *know* Castaldini will never be the same!"

"I could have told you that, without that historical kiss."

The four of them swung around to see Durante walking toward them, clapping, with a gigantic smile lighting up his impossibly handsome face. Leandro was a step behind, looking just as amused.

The two men immediately started ribbing Ferruccio mercilessly. He deflected their satire effortlessly, and the three men had her and the other two women laughing helplessly.

Clarissa marveled at how close those three were, how much in common they had. She knew he'd become Durante's friend, but had had no inkling how close they'd become. His closeness to Leandro was more puzzling. Her father had said he'd told a select few about Ferruccio's parentage when Ferrucio had first appeared in Castaldini. She doubted Leandro, who'd been exiled then, had been among them. Both of them were businessmen who played on the same level, so they might have known each other for years. But with everything she'd found out about Ferruccio in the past few days, she was convinced it had been he who'd sought out his relative. He'd wanted those of his family he liked and respected to be part of his life.

A surge of almost unbearable warmth and love welled inside her. He made it worse, as usual, gathering her to his side with such gentleness, breathing in the scent of her hair before planting a kiss on the top of her head. His action affected her far more when she realized he'd done it absently while totally involved in his verbal skirmish with her brother and cousin. It was as if he needed to touch her, to feel her close.

He gave her a squeeze before he let her go and turned to Luci.

Luci blinked up at him. Clarissa knew just what the poor girl was suffering from. Any female, no matter how loyal or how happy she was for her friend, would quiver at his merest look.

"Signorina Montgomery," Ferruccio said, looking serious all of a sudden. "Since all the people who matter to me are present, it's time to offer you my sincerest apologies for the inappropriateness I insulted you with on first meeting you."

Luci looked flustered for a second, then her face blazed with delight and deviltry. "Whoo boy, you remember?"

Clarissa groaned. "He forgets nothing, trust me."

"What's that all about?" Leandro asked.

"On his first appearance in the royal court," Luci revealed, imps of enjoyment dancing in her beautiful eyes, "he propositioned me *and* Stella before he even said hello or knew who we were. At the same time, if you get my drift."

Durante gaped at Ferruccio. "What? If anyone but both of you said this, I would have sworn on my right arm it was a lie. Were you under the influence of something foul that night or what?"

Ferruccio's gaze settled on Clarissa, becoming heavier by the second. "The most foul thing imaginable. I apologize to…all concerned."

Clarissa quivered inwardly. Was he apologizing to her, too? But Durante seemed convinced it was something ridiculously out of character for Ferruccio. So why had he done it? What was the "foul thing" that had made him act that way?

Before she could think further, Luci challenged, "All concerned? To Stella, too?"

He flicked a glance at the woman in question. She'd learned to keep her distance after Leandro had come down on her like a demolished building for daring to try to come between him and Phoebe. "I apologize only to human beings, not vipers."

Leandro burst out laughing. "You've found her out far faster than both me and Durante."

Ferruccio gave him a sage nod. "Compared to me, you've both led very sheltered lives."

Durante raised a formidable eyebrow. "Who're you calling sheltered?"

Ferruccio gave him a serene look. "Both of you, that's who."

Durante poked him in the chest. "Just for that, you're going to have to grovel a bit to get us to take the positions of your guardian angels on your new Council."

Leandro's grin turned evil. "Make that grovel *a lot.*"

Ferruccio maintained the same assurance. "I don't grovel. I'll just draft you into my service."

Leandro smirked. "Dream on, pal."

"And may they be happy dreams," Durante put in sarcastically. "Just for Clarissa's sake."

As they laughed, Gabrielle, Durante's new wife, glided up in the background like a butterfly, homing in on her husband, her face ablaze with pleasure as she watched him enjoying himself.

Clarissa had met her a couple of times before her and Durante's wedding, which had taken place before Clarissa had gone to the States for her mission.

She was the only one who'd noticed Gabrielle yet. And even though Gabrielle had eyes only for Durante, Clarissa started to smile. During their short meetings, she'd really liked the woman. She had great hopes that Gabrielle would turn out to be another great friend like Phoebe, her brother Paolo's sister-in-law, who was now Leandro's wife. And then, all Clarissa needed to love her was to see how happy Gabrielle made Durante.

Then she saw Gabrielle's eyes fall on Ferruccio.

Clarissa's heart faltered as Gabrielle's smile and steps did. It froze as she felt Ferruccio stiffen and turn his gaze to Gabrielle, as if he'd felt her approach, her reaction at seeing him. The same reaction filled his eyes.

Clarissa didn't know what it was. She only knew it was intense and instant. And it affected them both.

But it *didn't* feel like attraction.

Could she believe that, because it didn't feel like that to her? Or was she just deluding herself?

Confusion descended on her like a boulder as Gabrielle plastered her smile back on and hooked an arm through her husband's, rubbing against him like a delighted feline. With a rumble of welcome Durante caught her, shared as demonstrative a kiss with her as the one Clarissa and Ferruccio had just had.

Introductions to the new king-to-be ensued. The king-to-be whose eyes were still filled with something she hadn't suspected he was capable of as they surveyed her sister-in-law. Tenderness.

That shook her more than if she'd seen lust there.

Dio, what was this all about?

Soon the gathering disbanded, and he took her out to the verandah where they'd had their first fateful conversation.

She decided to get it out in the open. Before her head split open. She turned on him. "You liked Gabrielle, didn't you?"

He looked taken aback for a moment. Didn't think she'd notice, did he? Then he shrugged. "She's very nice." Then a slow, triumphant smile stretched his lips. "And you're very hot—even more arousing than usual if that's possible—when you're jealous."

"Are you trying to distract me?" she fumed.

"Only because you're barking up a light pole, not even the wrong tree. And I'd rather spend our time together doing something useful. Like discussing your wedding night lingerie."

"So I'm wrong?"

"Do you think you're right?" he countered. "Do you think I was hit by a bolt of attraction to your sister-in-law?"

"N-no," she admitted. "It didn't seem like attraction."

"Because it wasn't. You know firsthand what I'm like when I'm attracted—and with every other inch of your body. Gabrielle is lovely and it was as lovely to see how much she loves Durante, how much happiness they share."

The happiness we'll never share? she wanted to cry out. *Or is there hope for us? Your raging desire means something, doesn't it?*

Out loud she said, "So you were inspecting your friend's wife to see if she'd pass your specs?"

"She passed his specs. And then some. Like you do mine."

"D-do I? Do you really want this, Ferruccio?"

"I can show you right now what kind of…provisions I'm suffering beneath my tux so I won't walk around showing the world how much I *want* this, *mia bella unica.*" She gurgled as her eyes clung to the bulge that had conquered all his…provisions. "If you want…solid proof, I can waive my decree to wait until we're husband and wife, and unleash all the proof you need on your sanity-annihilating, potency-jeopardizing body. In fact, speaking of potency, maybe I'd better. Mine is in grave danger. Especially after that trick you pulled back there."

"You started it!"

"And I'm glad I did. You'll never cease to surprise me."

"Look who's talking!"

"I'm looking, and my insanity meter is nearing the red zone. So if you don't want the whole palace to stay awake all night hearing you scream with one orgasm after another—since the sound-proofing I'm installing in our apartments isn't yet complete—you should turn around and walk away now. And if you don't want me to pounce on you wherever I find you during the coming five days, you'd better stay out of my hunting grounds."

She gasped, turned around before *she* pounced on *him* and dragged him on top of her here and now.

He pulled her back. "Do you remember our first time out here?" She nodded, her head rolling against his muscle-padded shoulder. "I swore that one day I would make love to you in the exact spot where you stood and turned me down. And I will." He let her go so suddenly that she swayed. "Just not tonight. Now run, before my mind gives out and we end up giving the attendees of my first official reception something far more historically shocking than the most passionate kiss they ever saw."

She ran this time, her high heels clicking on the marble floor like the frantic heartbeats of an alien creature.

Before she could enter a quiet hall of the palace through an open French window, he called after her.

"For the wedding…layer on as much clothing as you can."

She turned around slowly. "Why? It's hot."

"It will be—as hot as you can survive." As she got his meaning, he was the one who turned around and walked away, like that first time, throwing over his shoulder, "Be as creative as you can be in the lingerie department. And most important of all, rest up, *mia bella unica*. You'll need all the stamina you can get from now on, now that you'll always be with me."

Defiance shot through her. She might have been only test driven, but she was now revving and raring to go. He shouldn't be the only one dealing out hormone-messing torment.

"Thanks for the instructions, my future liege," she chirped, pseudo-swooningly. She waited until he stopped, turned to face her, challenge rolling off him in waves. Then she let her voice heat, deepen, thicken. "Here are your future queen's instructions. No cologne or aftershave. I want to smell you. No…provisions. I want to feel your…proof. And though it won't make much of a difference in five days, don't get a haircut. Ever again. Until I tell you to. I want to feel my hands convulsing in a long, luxurious mane as you pleasure me."

Challenge became a shockwave of testosterone.

She turned and ran inside before it hit her, receded into the depths of the palace to the sound of his stunned, aroused, unbridled laughter.

Nine

"You do look like a queen!"

Clarissa stared at her reflection in the gilded, Rococco-style, antique full-length mirror. She had to admit that Antonia was right.

She felt like a new person, a real woman, a royal one, in this dress. It fit her like her skin did. No wonder. She'd stood for endless hours while a dozen designers had molded it around her.

But during the stages of its creation, she hadn't imagined how the finished product would look. Last she'd seen it, it had yet to be put together and embroidered. The result was… amazing.

Its second-skin bodice, with an off-shoulder neckline, accentuated curves she'd never noticed she possessed, nipped her waist to a sparseness she hadn't believed humanly possible—which remarkably wasn't achieved by a breath-depleting corset or contrast with a mushrooming skirt. The lack of the latter was Ferruccio's doing. "No parachutes," he'd decreed.

She'd fought against the "parachute" they'd planned for her to wear, until he'd ended the debate. Thankfully. Infuriatingly.

At least she now had what she'd petitioned for—a skirt that molded to her hips before flaring gently in layers made of the extra-light, bulk-free cloths Ferruccio had said should be allowed to touch her body. Chiffon, tulle, lace and, for public exposure purposes, a base of opaque silk. The whole dress was made up of these materials and was extensively adorned in pearls and transparent, rainbow-reflecting sequins. Those coalesced in the middle of her trimmed, scalloped skirt to form the crest of Castaldini.

She looked over her shoulder as Luci and Gabrielle hooked her twenty-foot train where it connected undetectably to the skirt. Also Ferruccio's doing. He'd demanded it be removable. Not that she had anywhere near enough layers to satisfy his expectations.

Well, he couldn't give her the mane she'd demanded, either. Not in just five days.

The ladies finished the tricky job and stood back, exclaiming over the beauty of the train. The heavily pregnant Phoebe applauded their efforts from a nearby sofa. Antonia came forward to add the final touch, the crown tiara of Castaldini.

Clarissa caught Antonia's tearful gaze in the mirror as she secured the tiara on top of her head. The heavily layered tulle veil flowed from the back of her chignon.

Clarissa knew that Antonia felt like the mother of the bride. Clarissa felt that she really was, too. But there was more to Antonia's distress than that. Not only was she seeing the daughter she'd hadn't given birth to getting married and crowned queen all at once, but she must be remembering the tragedy that had been Clarissa's mother's life, how different it could have been, how badly it had ended.

Her mother had worn this tiara, till she stopped appearing in public, around the time she'd gotten pregnant with Clarissa. Durante had insisted that Clarissa have it, had said that, when a new queen was crowned, he'd commission a replica to be made.

She'd told him she didn't want keepsakes, but he'd been adamant. She deserved to have something beautiful of their mother, a reminder of better times, when she'd been whole and had worn the crown with pride and grace.

She couldn't rebuff his thoughtfulness, misguided or not, and had taken the boxes containing this crown along with the rest of their mother's jewelry and personal treasures. She hadn't even opened them. She didn't ask who had, to get the crown out.

Now she was going to be the queen, and the crown was no longer just a keepsake. It was officially hers to wear.

Would her mother's misfortune go along with it?

Antonia placed her hands on her shoulders, squeezed, her breath uneven, her voice shaky. "Ah, *cara mia,* you are a vision."

Clarissa smirked at her in the reflection, so that her pillar-of-power nanny's poignancy wouldn't wreck her own fragile composure. "Clothes do make the woman, don't they? To your immense relief, I'm sure. You finally got me to look the part."

Antonia scowled, indignation palpable. "You *always* did. You always were the most beautiful, refined princess in the world."

"You tell her, Donna Antonia," Luci piped in, resplendent in her pale-gold gown with its corset-like bodice and full-bodied skirt. Yes, bridesmaids were allowed to wear parachutes. "I always said she was a true princess, unlike those affected, artificial types. But she never believed it. She has serious self-image issues, our girl. Where they originated from, I'll never understand."

Gabrielle sighed. "Ah, self-doubts. You never know what might form them. One thing is certain—every person you know has more to them that they let on or that you'll ever understand."

Wise woman, Clarissa thought. She'd never told Luci of the events of her childhood, so Luci had always been puzzled by what seemed inexplicable traits in Clarissa's character. Some had been as incomprehensible to Clarissa herself. She found the explanation to one now, as she gazed at herself in the mirror.

She'd thought pristine white would make her paleness look

sickly. Thinking that, she'd never worn white. In fact, she'd never given her looks much attention at all, believing there wasn't much to pay attention *to*. She now realized she'd been suffering from the sense of unworthiness that all who'd been abused as children suffer. It had made her unable to see her own assets.

She did now. She now noticed a golden tinge to her complexion, reflecting the hundred shades of her hair, and thought the white made her glow with vitality.

And she realized something more. It wasn't the effect of the dress. Ten days ago, its opulence and glamor would have only deepened her sense of gawkiness.

This new self-acceptance and assurance was all the magic of Ferruccio. The memory of his eyes and body worshipping every part of her. She now saw herself through his hunger and appreciation.

Suddenly a burst of sound shook the whole chamber.

It was the royal brass orchestra playing the royal anthem, heralding the beginning of the ceremonies. The coronation would start in twenty minutes. The wedding would follow immediately.

She turned around in panic. "Ladies, thank you for all your help. But can I please have a few minutes alone?"

"Our queen has spoken! Let's mosey on, folks." Luci winked at her as she and Gabrielle helped Phoebe up from the sofa. "You better not run away the moment our backs are turned, hear?"

Clarissa stuck out her tongue. But the moment the door closed behind them, she let her smile and shoulders droop.

Luci hadn't been completely joking. She felt Clarissa's turmoil, had assumed it was cold feet. If only Luci knew how hot her feet were. She wanted Ferruccio, wanted to be with him for as long as she lived with a ferocity that terrified her. Like he'd once said, she couldn't imagine a fall from this height.

She inhaled a steadying breath, neared the mirror.

She saw the difference in her that Luci had spoken of. The last of her naïveté and unawareness had been erased. There were no longer a girl's fears and uncertainties and suspicions in her eyes, but the openness of possibilities that limitless passion bestowed. The brand of a powerful male's possession showed in the intensity of her glance, the hunger in her lips. There was also a far deeper dread etched in her expression.

She did look different. She looked like a woman who had finally felt the range of emotions a woman could feel. A woman lost in love and fearing that love might remain lost to her forever.

She dropped her gaze to the necklace that lay heavy around her throat and chest, the centerpiece of the set Ferruccio had sent her, one of his wedding gifts.

In his note, he said he'd commissioned its creation for her from the top goldsmiths in Castaldini, who'd collaborated day and night to produce it in the past days.

The intricate design was a triumph of craftsmanship, a true resurrection of the ancient tradition of working in pure gold. The incredible luster, color and beauty of twenty-four carat gold made the piece even more incredible. She wondered how he'd gotten them to design it so that it would match the crown she'd wear, yet still have an individual look. And perfectly match her eyes.

Its foliate garlands were decorated with five hexagonal amethysts set within circular wreaths, alternating with pear-shaped scrolls. Everything was set with diamonds. According to the hefty certificate that had accompanied the set, the necklace alone had thirteen diamonds weighing seventy-five carats, sixty-nine smaller diamonds weighing fifty carats and numerous smaller rose-cut diamonds weighing twenty carats. The other pieces were earrings, a bracelet and a ring.

She couldn't even estimate how much they had cost. But a relative had once bragged that her five-carat diamond ring cost two hundred thousand U.S. dollars, so what she was wearing would probably plug Castaldini's financial deficit.

But cost was no issue to Ferruccio. What moved her was the thought he'd put into choosing the design, that he'd known how perfectly it would enhance her eyes and complexion and hair.

She had to believe that a man who'd given her that much pleasure, in so many ways, wouldn't end up destroying her.

And then, she wasn't a helpless bystander. Ferruccio had said her mother's expectations and actions had been at the root of her problems, that her attitude and surrender to her bitterness had exacerbated them. But Clarissa wasn't her mother. And she would love him as he deserved to be loved. He wanted her now—one day she might make him love her, too.

With that resolution bolstering her, she walked to the door, opened it. Her bridal party spilled in.

She laughed. "Oh, Luci! You really made them think I'd tear off my wedding gown, pull on black spandex and escape from the balcony using knotted sheets, didn't you?"

"The new you?" Luci snickered as she tidied Clarissa's veil. "I wouldn't put anything past you."

"Ladies, how about you get a move on?" Phoebe groaned. "If you keep me on my feet much longer, I'll have to watch both the coronation and the wedding from a TV in some maternity ward!"

"It's going to be a long day, Phoebe," Clarissa scolded, alarmed. "Quit being pigheaded and sit in the wheelchair!"

Grumbling that she wished them all to be in her condition soon, Phoebe complied.

Everyone laughed and rushed toward the throne room.

With every step, Clarissa felt that she was rushing toward her future. A future that for the first time she could visualize.

Lightheartedness and optimism suddenly flooded her.

She broke into a run.

Everyone burst out in excitement and ran after her.

The throne room was in fact a cathedral-size chamber that was a triumph of architecture. Its gigantic structure and one-hundred-foot-high domed ceiling seemed to have been built without pillars. The design married Moorish, Gothic and Baroque influences in perfect symbiosis and it boasted an extensive array of original Renaissance artwork by masters of the caliber of Raphael.

Clarissa thought the grandeur of the place was nothing, compared to that of the man who would today become its ruler.

She walked the twenty feet of her train ahead of her bridal procession, no bouquet in hand. She'd sent Ferruccio a note saying there wouldn't be one, and not to bother decreeing it. She wanted her hands free. He'd sent one back saying so did he.

She walked down the aisle among the hundreds of people congregated to witness the coronation, mostly nobles and members of the extensive D'Agostino royal family. She had to sit at the front row. After the king was crowned, it was Castaldinian custom that his queen be summoned to sit beside him on the throne.

For long years, while her mother lived, her seat had remained empty. It had been removed altogether when she died five years ago. It had been a year after Clarissa had finished college. But with Ferruccio in the picture then, and her escaping regularly back to the States on the pretext of starting postgraduate studies, she'd always wondered if her absence, both real and emotional, had been what had finally driven her mother over the edge.

She shook herself as she reached the front row. Today belonged to the present, to the future. No more dwelling on the past.

Her party hurried to sit down as trumpets blared again, heralding Ferruccio's arrival. From the corner of her eye she saw Leandro rushing over to scoop Phoebe from the wheelchair, taking her to the back of the pews where she could stretch out.

Then everything disappeared. Only he was left. Ferruccio.

The man she loved, had loved since she'd first seen him.

He entered the chamber from its northern end, walked in long, powerful strides toward the platform housing the thrones.

She'd seen the traditional black-with-gold-trim coronation costume, with its Roman-Moorish design and embroidery, its crimson sash and hanging sword in dozens of paintings on dozens of kings, her father among them. On Ferruccio it was different.

The clothes didn't make the man, after all. In his case, it was the other way around. If he'd looked like a god before, he now looked like a superhero god.

The eleven o'clock sunlight poured over him from the stained-glass windows high on the walls, making his skin glow, his raven hair glint, every thread of gold on his costume gleam with sparkles of magic. Deepening the impression was the crimson cape of kingship, with Castaldini's crest emblazoned in gold, that hung from his shoulders and flowed down his back. He looked daunting, majestic, a man born to be lord of all he surveyed.

As he approached, a movement to the side caught her eye.

Durante and Paolo were helping their father to his feet. He'd now perform another first in Castaldinian history. An abdication.

No new king had ever been crowned while the old one lived.

The head of the Council headed toward the king's throne to perform the transfer of power and the coronation rituals.

Her breath caught in her lungs as all the players converged toward the momentous event.

Then Ferruccio diverged from the path.

He left them all staring after him in total loss.

She sat there, her every muscle slack as he approached her with those inexorable steps.

He stopped right above her. Her breathing stopped, as well.

He bent, took her clammy hands, bowed deeply, planted a kiss on the back of each hand, then into her palms. She was quaking by the time he straightened. "Shall we, *regina mia?*"

His queen! "B-but you have to be crowned first."

"I'm going to be king in minutes. I say what happens first. First you sit were you belong, on the throne. Then I join you."

He was talking quietly, intensely. But she knew everyone around her had heard him. Judging by the buzz that swept the chamber like a gigantic swarm of bees, everyone had. Luci was suppressing giggles and fanning herself with exaggerated speed.

Ferruccio seemed unaware of anything or anyone but her, his eyes on her like a tractor beam, making her float beside him to the platform. He led her up the five marble steps that were covered in a crimson carpet printed with Castaldini's crest.

At the queen's throne, he stopped, the intensity in his eyes rising as he pressed her hands. "This is your throne, Clarissa. This is your crown, too. Yours alone."

She didn't get it for a moment. Then comprehension exploded.

It was…too much to believe. He *couldn't* have. Could he? How? When? Why? And she choked out, "You mean…?"

He pressed her hands harder. "I had them made for you. Everything is yours, Clarissa, no one else's."

This wasn't the throne her mother had sat on. This wasn't the crown she'd worn. He'd known. He'd understood. How she'd feel that they were tainted by turmoil and unhappiness. And he'd made her new ones, free of the blot of the past.

She collapsed onto her throne. Her king's gift. Of a pure and new beginning, of a future all her own to write.

It was too much. What he was. What he kept giving her.

Surely this meant she wasn't just his convenient bride, if he'd go to these lengths to anticipate her desires, to circumvent and negate her anxieties and discomforts?

He bent and kissed her eyelids as she had his that night he'd claimed her, driving her nightmares away as she had his.

He crooked her a smile. "The sooner I get the formalities out of the way, the sooner you can show me how creative you've been."

A smile trembled on her lips as he walked away. Tears filled her down to the roots of her being, with gratitude so fierce it was exquisite agony. They flowed down her cheeks throughout the magical moments, as she watched the men who were the pillars of her life secure the future of her beloved Castaldini, as her father, passed the power and the responsibility to the man who most deserved it. Her lover. Her king. And within this day, her husband.

"*Dio,* who are all these people?" Clarissa squinted up into the extensive, packed, semicircular Roman theatre.

It was built into the hillside overlooking the royal palace, had stood there neglected for as long as she'd lived. Now it looked as good as new, bursting with lavish Roman-Moorish decorations, with thousands of guests milling around the sloping, steplike seats. Not to mention countless scurrying photographers from media agencies from around the world, and cameramen transmitting the wedding on global live feed.

Every detail had been brought into existence by Ferruccio's vision and orchestration, in the six days he'd specified.

He turned to her with a smile rivaling the summer afternoon's sun. "Those are your relatives and subjects, *regina mia.*"

"The relatives are yours now, too. And the subjects are yours *first,* mine only by association. They're here because you invited them. You see those six ladies over there?" She pointed to her friends, who burst to their feet waving and hooting. She waved as enthusiastically back. "They are my contribution to the crowds."

"I know. Your friends from your college and postgraduate years." She blinked at him. He knew? No, he *more* than knew.

"You did something, didn't you?"

He waved to the ladies, who swooned down to their seats. "I took the liberty of returning the plane tickets you bought them, sent them my jet instead."

Her mouth fell open. "*Dio,* Ferruccio. The things you keep doing. I don't know whether to be delighted or alarmed."

"Be delighted. I'll never suffocate you or railroad you."

"Really? Strange. I remember you doing some of the first and a lot of the second in very recent memory."

His smile froze. She wanted to kick herself in the teeth.

Why had she said that? Those had been the sentiments she'd hidden behind until she faced the truth.

The truth was that she would have never agreed to marry him if she hadn't been dying to anyway. More important, she believed he would have never coerced her, would have let her go.

And if a voice taunted her that he still might some day, she couldn't and wouldn't listen to it.

"I thought we were past the hostilities, that you've accepted our situation, saw the good in it." He waited for her answer, but protests and explanations clogged in her throat. He seemed to misunderstand her frustrated stare. His voice thickened. "I wanted to make the best of it, to do things for you that only I can."

That was what he was doing? Making the best of the situation?

Suddenly the euphoria and optimism that had fueled her for the past hours drained out of her system, left her feeling helpless, hopeless. "And you can do anything, can't you?"

His eyes grew darker as they roamed her. "Not everything, no."

After that, they sat in silence on the thrones he'd transported there, until the royal guards converged at the back of the stage, heralding the arrival of Castaldini's cardinal.

Suddenly Ferruccio broke their silence, giving her a look soaked in challenge. "How appropriate it is to marry you here, Clarissa. Where else would a man marry a lioness but in a place where in ancient times gladiators fought lions for their lives?"

Her heart fluttered as she pounced on the opening, prayed her teasing tone and smile would show him there was no rancor left in her. "It was also in such places that sacrifices were tossed to predators like you to devour."

His answering smile told her he'd read her meaning, her mood, was delighted by both. "So, my sacrifice, which part of you would your recommend I devour first?"

She filed her nails against her bodice. "So, my gladiator, which part of you would you like me to shred to ribbons first?"

He laughed, heaved up to his feet, swooped down on her and dragged her to hers. "Come, *leonessa mia,* let the duel begin."

The cardinal came to stand before them, turning his back to the crowd so that they faced their subjects-to-be.

With everyone silent and with the acoustic structure of the theater, as soon as the cardinal raised his voice to recite the Castaldinian wedding vows, it was as if he was speaking into a sound-amplifying system.

He paused, waiting for Ferruccio to repeat the words after him. Ferruccio just gestured for him to go on.

Looking shocked, but not about to argue with his new king on global live feed, the man went on. But when he came to the part where he had to ask the questions answered by "I do"s, Ferruccio stopped him. Clarissa was as much at a loss as the poor man.

Ferruccio turned to her. "I've parroted enough pledges today. But this is one pledge I'm making on my own." Then he raised his voice. "Do you Clarissa D'Agostino, my lioness, my queen, my savior from the darkness, want me to be your defense and harbor, your support and succor, your ally and lover?"

She stared at him. *Too much* rang in her mind in a loop.

She had one answer.

She surged into him, hugged him with all her strength.

He hugged her back, exhaled as if he'd been bating his breath, whispered to her only, "Then take all of me, *mia bella unica.*"

The crowd treated them to a standing ovation.

After the tumult his unorthodox wedding vows had caused had died down, and they were again sitting in their thrones with her trembling so hard that she could barely sit up, she saw Ferruccio staring sideways. She followed his gaze.

Her heart twitched when she found it settled on Gabrielle. Gabrielle looked back at him and he gave her a conspiratorial wink.

Before Clarissa's heart could thud with alarm, Gabrielle turned and clung to Durante, seemed to be pleading with him. Durante kept shaking his head until she pouted. He sighed in what looked like defeat, stood up, mock-scowled down on her, then turned and walked toward the stage. Gabrielle gave Ferruccio a bursting-with-excitement smile. He gave her the thumbs-up.

Clarissa had never been so confused.

Durante climbed onto the stage, growled for their ears only, "You're paying for this, Ferruccio. Big time."

She grabbed Ferruccio's arm. "What's going on?"

He smiled. "Watch. Or more accurately, listen."

Durante faced the crowds. "This is for my sister and queen, Clarissa." He tossed a 'take that' look back at Ferruccio. Ferruccio retaliated with one bedeviling eyebrow wiggle. Durante narrowed his eyes then turned around.

And started to sing.

Sing? Durante? Had the world tilted on its axis?

Clarissa didn't realize her mouth was hanging wide open until Ferruccio's gentle caress closed it for her.

She looked back at him, flabbergasted. He'd known Durante could sing, had set it up with Gabrielle to give her this, the gift of hearing her brother singing for the first time in her life. And boy, could Durante sing! He was *incredible.*

By the time Durante finished the aria "Nessun Dorma"—none shall sleep tonight—from the opera *Turandot* by Puccini, and bowed to a storming-with-applause crowd, Clarissa was bawling.

She burst to her feet, zoomed across the stage and grabbed Durante in a rib-crushing hug. As he hugged her back, Clarissa saw their father, openly in a wheelchair now, watching them with his cheeks wet. The crowd roared, demanding an encore, with Paolo and Julia leading the petitions.

As Durante succumbed and sang something more lighthearted from *Le Nozze di Figaro,* by Mozart, Ferruccio came behind her, took her leaning back into him, as they listened along with the rapt crowd.

She was still weeping her joy as Durante finished his second aria and wouldn't be prevailed upon for more curtain calls.

Her brother turned to her, kissed her. Then, as he shook Ferruccio's hand, he grabbed him nearer, gave him a lethal smile. "King or no king, best friend or not, Ferruccio, if I don't see my sister bouncing with happiness, you're a dead man."

Ferruccio gave him an inexplicable smile before turning his eyes to Clarissa. "My life depends on you now."

She wanted to say, if it were up to her, he'd live forever.

She didn't, and after Durante went back to his wife and Ferruccio took her back to their thrones, she could only sit there, reverberating with the enormities that Ferruccio had put her through throughout the day.

He leaned close, took her trembling hand. “I wish I could have been the one to sing for you, but if you’re looking for things I can’t do, singing tops the list.”

She wanted to tell him he’d given her far more than she could ever express. She knew if she did, she’d burst into tears again and this time wouldn’t stop.

She gave him a tremulous smile instead. “It’s okay. Lions aren’t known for their singing ability. You roar and rumble and purr pretty good, though.”

His eyes ignited as he got to his feet, sweeping her up with him. “Time to haul you to my lair, *leonessa mia.*”

Ten

On the short "haul" to Ferruccio's "lair," he drowned her in exhilaration and arousal, every second solidifying the spell he'd woven around her with that first glance.

He took her inside the mansion, kissed her deeply as he took off her veil, shook down her hair, but kept her crown on. Then he almost drove her out of her mind taking off her train.

She was wondering if he'd take her right there in the lounge, when he straightened, kissed her on the nape, then walked away.

After ten minutes, she called out to him. He didn't answer.

Confusion was starting to turn into panic that he'd fallen, hit his head and couldn't hear her, when she noticed what was in front of her all the time. A huge box, exquisitely wrapped in violets, with a matching envelope on top.

She pounced on it, taking longer than her nerves could stand, preserving the wrapping. Then she snatched open the lid.

Inside was a folded lavender paper. He had everything in her favorite colors.

She unfolded it. His handwriting. She felt as if he was whispering the words in her ear.

> "I'm resurrecting the Castaldinian ancient custom of *prima notte di nozze nascondino*. But this wedding night hide-and-seek has a twist to it. Instead of the groom pursuing the bride, you, *leonessa,* champion runner bride of mine, will pursue me. I've done my share of the running for six years, after all."
>
> "Did you think I was going to let you off the hook?"

She could almost hear his teasing, feel his hands and lips trailing a path of sensual torment all over her secrets and hungers, before he stepped away, left her gasping for more.

> "But since I'm not a merciless, shameless siren, I'll give you clues, so you can catch me."
>
> "My first clue is: Where did I first claim you?"

She was zooming up the stairs to his bedroom, when she faltered. He'd really claimed her with that first kiss.

She could be wrong, but what was the worst thing that could happen? She'd return to his bedroom to find her clue.

But she believed she was right.

She took off her high-heeled sandals, hooked them in one hand, gathered the layers of her skirt in the other and ran out, following the same route he'd taken her on that first night.

She again reveled in the feel of sand below her naked soles, wished he was there running with her.

She arrived at the spot of their waveside dinner, found the circle of brass poles blazing. In its middle, instead of their table, she found a huge mother-of-pearl sea snail shell.

She snapped it up, found her next clue.

> "How did you know where I was the night I made you mine?"

The answer came to her at once this time. She'd headed west.

She headed west now.

The more distant she was from the mansion and the fire and the darker it got, the more the gibbous moon blazed to illuminate the night. Then she saw it in the distance. A path of flame-lit lanterns. She gathered her skirt higher and ran.

The trail ended at stone steps winding around the foot of the mountain she'd seen from the mansion. She'd run that far? Good thing she was in shape.

She scaled the wide steps, knowing now why he'd said no parachutes. Wearing one of those inflated skirts, she could have launched off the mountain with the strong gusts of breeze. There was also no way she could have climbed them in a permanent train.

Then she reached the top of the winding steps and finally saw her destination. An observatory-like building.

The huge edifice stood framed against the rising moon, making her feel as if she'd stumbled into a scene from a Gothic romance.

Which wasn't far from the truth. She was rushing to her tormented, tormenting, irresistible, all-powerful lover.

She ran to the door, found it ajar. She entered, adrenaline rushing through her blood. She'd never felt so excited. So alive. One more unprecedented experience he'd given her.

And it was only beginning.

She put her sandals on again and followed the light.

With every step she felt she was wading deeper into another waking dream, as she reached the beginning of a path cleared between the candles he had crowding every surface imaginable.

Then the candles ended abruptly, and she found her next clue on top of a big brass lantern in the middle of the next dark hall.

"Now, follow what is your name."

Her name. Clarissa meant bright or brilliant. But there was only darkness from here on. What else emitted light?

The moon. But how did she follow it inside here?

It came to her. She had to find windows. As long as she saw the moon from them, she was on the right track.

She found the windows, followed the moon. That led her to another chamber filled with candles, almost surrounded by open, floor-to-ceiling windows letting in the night breeze that kept the hundreds of tiny flames flickering. A huge bed spread in dark satin that she was sure was violet was at the far end by the western windows. By the eastern ones, there was a dinner set up like the one they'd had by the sea.

He walked in from the verandah. Her Roman god come to life.

"I knew you were brilliant, in every way."

His voice cascaded over her, intertwining with the composite music of the night. The sea's rushing and receding tempo, the wind's whistling sighs, tranquility's still song.

He prowled toward her slowly, so slowly across the expansive space, giving her a hormone-roaring show of contained power and inbred poise in his king's regalia. She couldn't bear it, started to run to him. He raised a hand, stopped. She stopped, too, starting to shake with the pressure of craving.

"Take that work-of-art wrapping off for me, *regina mia.* It's done its purpose, tantalized and maddened me all day by how it worships your beauty, caresses and kisses and clings to your flesh when I couldn't. It has overstayed its welcome."

"Don't—don't you want to take it off me?"

"Undressing you is now my main mission in life, along with possessing and pleasuring you, but I'm feeling almost hostile toward the thing. I might not be considerate of the imbalance of power between us if I wrestle it off."

"There'll be no wrestling. It's easy to take off. That *was* one of your demands." Excitement and the blaze of appreciation and lust in his eyes made her brazen. She twisted around, leaned to make her hair spill forward, presenting him with a clear shot of her back, widening her stance and thrusting her hips at him slightly in provocation. "Down the zipper goes, and the dress follows."

His rumble harmonized with that of the sea. "Or I can just

flip up that skirt, bend you over and give you what you're asking for." She almost fell to her knees begging him for it. "And I will. Sometime during the night, I'll put you back into that virginal torture device and ride you like that until you faint with pleasure again. All in good time. The best."

The fire in her loins was spreading, consuming her. Gush after gush of readiness was now flooding down her thighs. And all he'd done was expose her to his visual and verbal desire. He could talk about torture. He was a connoisseur at it, after all.

"Now show me the miracle of you."

She opened her mouth to ask him for help. The back zipper had needed an extra pair of hands to do it up. She clamped her lips. He wanted her to undress for him on her own. And she was doing it.

She reached back and managed to yank the zipper down in a feat of agility she hadn't known she was capable of. Unbearable hunger was an unstoppable motivator, a miracle worker. The dress spilled off her arms. She caught it before it pooled to the ground.

"Let it go, Clarissa. Let me see what ingenious lingerie you've got underneath."

She let it go.

Ferruccio stared. And stared.

He'd told her to be creative. He hadn't imagined anything like that.

"This was the most creative thing I could come up with."

He shuddered at the mixture of uncertainty and brazenness in her voice. Why uncertain? She wasn't sure how this affected him? She didn't know he'd never again open his eyes or close them and see anything but the sight before him now?

Her. Standing tall and proud and annihilating in her transparent high heels and the jewels he'd had made for her, in the middle of a dream of glittering white. Totally naked.

He wanted to hurtle to her, slam into her, squeeze and

devour every inch of her. He rocked on his heels under the force of the compulsion. But he wanted to savor the sight of her more, her counterattack on his reason, see her coming to him, bent on pulverizing it, on beating him at his game of seduction.

"An ingenious choice of…*un-wear, regina mia.*" He beckoned to her. She stepped out of her pooled dress, prowled toward him, her beauty intensifying with every step. He licked his tingling lips, almost feeling them on her shiny lips, on her other now equally smooth ones. "Unique and unrepeatable."

"Glad you approve." She entered the circle of moonlight, stopped. He rumbled, prodding. She was half-a-dozen steps away.

She stood her ground. "Show *me* your magnificence, *re mio.*"

His first impulse was to tear at his clothes like a demented man. He called on the remnants of a control he'd once thought unassailable and unhooked his cape. He swung it over his shoulders like a matador, before giving it a swirl and tug, bringing it spooling around his forearm.

She whooped, clapped. "Do it again!"

His lips spread in delight at seeing hers. "Glad you approve. But there will be only one thing I do again—and again—tonight."

Her pose grew languid, seductive and shy all at once.

He took off his sash and sword, undid his jacket a button a second, dropped it to the floor. His dress shirt followed. The moment his hands went to his pants she ran to him.

She grabbed his hands, stopping them. "My turn."

His eyes glazed over her as she dropped to a crouch before him. The sight of the ripe swell of her buttocks, the graceful curve of back, her gleaming skin and sparkling hair almost drove him over the edge. She pulled his pants down, causing his engorged manhood to rebound against his belly, throbbing, straining.

She tried to touch him, but he stepped away and out of his pants, kicked away his shoes and got rid of his socks. Then he did what he'd wanted to do ever since he'd first seen her.

He bent and hauled her over his shoulders.

She gasped as he swept her across the chamber, crossed into the wide circle of candles and lanterns around the bed that he'd placed by the open windows overlooking the sheer side of the mountain and the sea. Her panting became moans, then he felt her lips latching on to his shoulder blade, her teeth sinking there. He roared, ran the last steps, flipped her over onto the bed, watched her bounce on the dark violet sheets, a goddess of sensual decadence and dementia, bidding him come lose his mind.

He obeyed, came down over her, filling her outstretched arms.

She grabbed his head as his lips branded their way from her neck to her nipples. "Sorry I couldn't layer more clothes."

He raised his head. "Sorry I couldn't grow my hair faster."

She buried her nose in his chest, inhaled his unadorned scent. "But you followed my other instructions. I say we call it even."

"I say we call it even better. Than our first night."

"There could be nothing better. I just want encores."

"Ah, Clarissa, you force me to sound condescending, but you have no idea. The pleasure I gave you was only an appetizer. Now I will give you a…full meal."

"Oh? And how are you sure of that?"

"I'm going by the fact that you were in a measure of pain then. Now, it will all be pleasure."

"Show me."

"I will. Always." He rose, bent to run his lips and tongue over her breasts, her abdomen, lower, bringing her to the edge before retreating, until she was begging for his invasion. He held back, came up, captured one nipple after the other, drawing soft, then hard, had her thrashing with each pull.

She sabotaged his reason, surging into him, bringing him full over her, taking his weight, containing him in hunger-driven limbs that clamped him, body and will. Her fingers caressed his flesh, unraveled his control, her lips, full and fragrant, pressed against his, her tongue invading his mouth, flooding him with her taste and her passion, turning the kiss into a full rehearsal of the mating they'd soon lose themselves in.

He tore his lips from hers, growled at the separation, at the convulsion that went through her, saw his insanity reflected in the depths of eyes gone purple. He shuddered in unison with her as arousal turned into agony.

"I can't bear it…just thrust inside me."

He had to face it. He couldn't wait. Not this first time. And she couldn't either. He'd give them this, the first explosive release that would free them to explore the fathomless depths of their passion with the leisure it deserved.

He reached for the side table and grabbed one of the foil packets he'd placed in a bowl, which sat among the colorful array of wine, brandy and water bottles and crystal glasses.

"Don't." She stayed his hand as he began to open the condom.

His eyes clung to hers, as if he could read her mind if he looked into them intensely enough. Had she installed her own protection?

Whatever the reason, she wanted to feel him without barriers again. Wanted to feel him pour his seed inside her. And that was the biggest gift, the only real one he felt he'd ever received.

He threw the condom away and crashed his lips on hers.

She jerked, wailed into his mouth, "Just fill me."

He rose between her splayed thighs, probed her with a finger, then two. She was flowing for him. He soothed her frenzy, trying to rein in his own, took her buttocks in one hand, tilted her to him as his other hand roamed her, in wonder, in ownership. He brought his shaft to her scorching entrance, rested there, struggling with the elemental need to plunge hard, seek her depths, go home. There would be no rush this time. No pain.

"Take your fill of me, *regina mia.*" Gritting his teeth, he began to invade her, the beauty open before him, her constant pleas a current fusing his insides.

He went blind with the burst of pleasure, at the heat and slickness and tightness of the velvet vise enveloping him. He stilled in her depths as she arched off the bed at his invasion.

"*Perdonami, amore mio,*" he rasped in his agitation.

She panted. "Forgive you? For what?"

"For not taking you with more restraint the first time."

She thrust her hips up. "I didn't want you to be restrained. That's why it didn't occur to me to tell you you were my first."

"And *only.*" He thrust, stamping his claim deeper. She swooned beneath him, opening wider, accepting anything he'd do to her. "You're mine and mine alone. But it didn't matter that you didn't tell me. I should have noticed, should have felt your pain. Damn me, I thought it was extreme pleasure."

"It was. The pain merged into pleasure and was…incredible."

"Whatever pain I caused you, I'll make it up to you, in a lifetime of pure and intensifying pleasures."

"I don't know if I can survive more pleasure than that." Her fingers dug into his chest, his shoulders, bringing him down to her, forcing him to stroke deeper into her. She cried out, a hot sharp sound of exultation that tore a growl of pride out of him.

She thrashed her head, never taking her eyes off his, letting him see every sensation rip through her, the thousand shades of gold in her hair, her golden paleness brightening with her rising pleasure, burning up the darkness she lay on, an image the old masters would have paid in blood to capture unto eternity.

"You feel…magnificent…inside me…" Her voice was smoky, exhilaration thickening it, sending another tidal wave of arousal crashing through him. "I never imagined so much pleasure existed. Give me all of you, as you promised, *amore,* take all of me."

The word *amore* gasped with such conviction, burst in his mind, in his heart, with such acute surprise, such pleasure that he almost keeled over.

He rose on extended arms, surveyed her feverishly. She looked every inch a woman in a tumult of…love? Or had it just been an endearment fueled by pleasure and the maddening need for release?

He'd take anything. Need could become love.

He fed her hunger for more of him, struggling as the slide inside her gripping heat sliced through him. He wanted this to last.

He watched in awe as she accepted all of him, wild, abandoned. Then she was weeping as she sought his lips, her core throbbing around him, demanding him harder, faster. He had to obey her.

His plunging rhythm became pounding, until her cries rose to a shriek that ripped through him. She arched up, convulsed in a full-body fit that shredded her cries, wrenched at his shaft. The knowledge that he was fulfilling her tore his own climax from depths he'd never known existed.

With a prayer that his seed would take root in her womb, he jetted inside her, causing her paroxysm to spike. Detonations of ecstasy rocked him, and her, locked them in a closed circuit of overstimulation, dissolved them into each other.

When it felt his heart would never restart, the tumult gave way to the warmth and weakness of satiation. He felt her melt beneath him, awe and fulfillment glowing on her face.

"Moglie mia, regina mia," he rumbled against her lips as he twisted, bringing her on top of him, maintaining their connection.

She pressed her lips to his heart. *"Marito mio, re mio."*

Her answering proclamation confirming him her husband and king, roared through his blood with pride and relief. Resurging desire, too, since she spoke in that new voice of hers, the one she now used only with him, awareness-laden, smug, overcome.

She raised her head, her hair draping over his chest. She gave him such a smile, no inhibitions, awakened, gaining in confidence. She would be annihilating when she realized her full power. He couldn't wait to be devastated. "You're always right, aren't you? I thought our first time was magic. Now I've given up trying to come up with descriptions. No language can do justice to what you do to me, what you give me."

He stroked her, moved, grateful, bursting with pride and joy. "It's the same with me."

Her gaze faltered. "You don't have to say that. Your experience—"

He cut her off, needing her to know, to never doubt. "Is obscenely overrated. And irrelevant. You would understand, if you had any. You would realize that what you knew as sex is nothing when you can experience *this*." He crushed her whole length to him. "Raging, blinding, transfiguring passion."

She cried out at his intensity, her face blazing with emotion at his confession, her body blossoming under his hunger, undulating in a renewed dance of sinuous demand and submission.

He rose, swung her up in his arms. She clung to him as if she was a part of him as he took her to the next phase he had prepared in her seduction and sensual enslavement. And his.

He'd given her that ride he'd promised her, under a canopy by the lapping waves. Then he'd stripped her of her torture device of a dress and taken her into the warm waters, driven her over many edges there. *Then* he'd wrapped her in silk and carried her back to their mansion. He'd taken her again in the swimming pool. Then she'd taken him, dissolved him in her hands and mouth. It had been another first for him, surrendering control to that extent.

Now she was curled into him, replete and depleted, a smile painting her face even in sleep, taking her beauty to a new level.

If their first night had been earthshaking, their wedding night had been life-changing.

She had changed his life in the past ten days. Changed *him.* Beyond recognition. And he liked the man she'd changed him into. He could finally be at peace with that man.

And that man couldn't wait to experience every second of their deepening passion, to surrender to the magic that bound them.

Clarissa watched Ferruccio answer one phone call and put two on hold as he signed the papers that Alfredo flipped over for him.

It was a financial treaty with a neighboring kingdom. He

hadn't had time to read the fine print, and she'd stepped in, in her role as financial advisor and analyst, gone over it with a fine-toothed comb and recommended that he sign. He refused the very idea of her double-checking her verdict. She'd fallen in love with him a bit more over that. If that was humanly possible.

For the past six weeks Ferruccio had been embroiled in the duties of his new status, putting right so many things that had gone wrong long before her father had fallen ill. He'd told her he'd been able to do so much in that time frame because he'd had her help and counsel. He seemed to revel in their interaction as much as she did, their synergy, in matters of state. And on every other level.

He now gestured for her that he'd take the phone calls and catch up with her, and she walked out to their apartments.

As she entered the place that had previously been an unused wing in the palace, which he'd transformed into their own world of ecstasy and intimacy, she found herself holding her breath.

She was almost always holding her breath, with dread that something might happen to shatter the perfection.

Ferruccio had turned out to be far more than she'd ever dreamed. He was a better king than her father had been, and she didn't feel disloyal thinking that. It was simply the truth.

He was the right man at the right time, giving Castaldini the stability it needed, introducing innovations with utmost care, while making certain to maintain its uniqueness and traditions, and to protect it from the infringement of harmful outside influences.

The one thing she'd thought marred his character, the chunk of steel he had for a heart, was nowhere to be found. As a liege he was approachable and just, as a new member of an extensive family where many had accepted him only as a dire fate, he was tolerant, patient, even amused. As a lover and husband he was…indescribable.

She kept wondering, could this be real? Or was he only

making the best of it, as he'd told her during their wedding? To keep the future mother of his children happy to stay in the marriage? But if he kept on being this incredible to her, should she even care about his motives or his true emotions?

She hadn't done anything about protection, for fear of harming the baby that could have been forming inside her. She'd also wanted to have full intimacy with him, and wanted all this pleasure to bear fruit.

It hadn't. She'd had a period.

He hadn't said anything, but she felt his disappointment. He really wanted a child. Probably more.

What if she couldn't give him one? What would happen if, after the time he'd specified had elapsed, she still hadn't? Would he decide their marriage wasn't a "viable endeavor" and cast her out of his life? Could she survive if he did?

She felt sick with uncertainty.

She sat down, leaned over until her head was almost between her knees. The world spun in a purple vortex.

"Clarissa!"

She jerked up, but her blood didn't follow. Everything blinked out.

It blinked back again. Ferruccio was kneeling before her, propping her up. She'd fainted. She didn't know how he'd reached her in time to prevent her collapse to the ground. Her superhero.

"Clarissa, *amore,* you're sick!"

She waved away his diagnosis. "I'm just missing a few hours of sleep. You know, those I regularly forgo to feast on Your Mouthwatering Majesty."

His lips compressed. "I'm calling in a doctor."

Her objections that she was fine fell on perfectly formed, selectively deaf ears.

Twenty minutes later, she was in bed being prodded by five royal physicians. She was sure there was nothing wrong with her. But it *was* bliss to be fussed over by Ferruccio like this.

Even if he was only concerned about the health of the potential mother of his child?

She sighed again as she lay back for the exam.

Yes, even then.

Ferruccio sank his fingers in his newly grown hair, almost pulling it out.

He'd been constantly wondering whether Clarissa really no longer considered him beneath her. If she really didn't think him a marauder, a usurper. If she'd truly forgotten their original deal, wanted to continue their marriage because it was all working so spectacularly.

Everything had been flowing so much like a dream that he'd been constantly dreading some rude awakening. But all his anxieties paled into nothing compared to the dread that ate at him now. He would welcome anything now, would be willing to lose her in any way but something happening to her. He'd give up everything, his very life, to make her whole.

"King Ferruccio."

He turned around, looking at the five men as if they were monsters he would take apart at the slightest wrong move. *That* move would be to tell him anything was wrong with Clarissa.

"King Ferruccio, are you all right?"

"Shut up," he snarled. "Talk."

The men looked more confused and more than a little alarmed, until one seemed to understand, came forward, his expression that of someone bearing news he knew he'd be obscenely rewarded for. "Congratulations, Your Majesty. The queen is pregnant."

Ferruccio stared at the man as if he'd just told him the queen was really a man. Then he growled, "What are you talking about? She's just had a period!"

This time none of the men were fazed. Another doctor ventured to approach. "That does sometimes happen during the first couple of months of pregnancy. But it means nothing, and it doesn't affect the pregnancy in the least."

Ferruccio's world emptied. His mind. His heart. And then, one thing filled them all. Clarissa. Everything to him. And now, impossibly, more than everything. She'd already given him everything. Now she'd give him more. *Pregnant.*

"By our calculations, the queen must have conceived on your wedding night."

Ferruccio's gaze swam around, registering the men with the last working faculty in his mind, seeing the male kudos in their eyes at the proof of his virility.

Then he no longer saw them. Everything disappeared from his awareness except one thing. A conviction. He *knew* Clarissa had conceived that first time they'd claimed each other.

Then he was hurtling through their apartments on a tidal wave of joy, sending a pile of paper scattering as if zapped by a whirlwind. He was. A whirlwind of boundless bliss and eternal gratitude.

His Clarissa would give him a miniature of her to adore.

He slowed down as he entered their room. She might not be sick, but she wasn't feeling well. How thoughtless would it be to explode into the room like a delirious dog, oblivious of her state and bound only on slurping her up in his hyperexcitement?

Good thing she hadn't seen him yet. She lay on the bed facing away from the door. She hadn't heard him, either, not with the ultrathick carpets he'd strewn the place with so they could make love anywhere and everywhere. *Grazie a Dio.* Outside, he'd sounded—and must have looked—like a one-man riot.

He started crossing the room and…stopped. Froze. Impaled on the spear that had stabbed him through the heart.

*Dio santo…*Clarissa…she…looked bereft.

She didn't want the baby? Because it was his?

Basta! Stop it…you fool. *Dio solo sa*—God only knew what she was feeling now, physically. A woman pregnant for the first time, in that delicate first trimester, with all its physiological adjustments, when she'd had to deal with so much during the past weeks. The wedding and coronation, the enormous workload she'd imposed on herself. But the real tests had been the emotional upheavals he'd put her through, the unrelenting physical demands he made on her, as she'd told him just an hour ago. He was the cause of her distress the way he'd been… *Dio,* he hadn't even asked those doctors if he should…

Her sob fractured his thoughts. His world.

Clarissa…no…*prego*…please…don't…

She didn't hear his mental pleading. She started sobbing as if her heart had splintered, was tearing the rest of her apart.

She hated it, the child that was growing inside her. Couldn't bear to have it invading her flesh, drawing from her life. Just because it was his child, too. Because she hated him.

He staggered. Nothing…*nothing* in his miserable, violent life had hit anywhere near this hard. Every injury he'd sustained had made him stronger. This…this finished him.

Something agonizing forged like white-hot skewers through his brain, poured like molten lead down his face, scorching his flesh and soul. He didn't know what it was. Didn't care.

Time distorted into a monstrous dimension more hideous than his worst nightmare.

Then it ceased. He didn't know when or where he was. Just that he was leaning against a wall, feeling like a building about to collapse, and his eyes were burning and wet. Tears?

But he'd never shed them. After all he'd been through, he'd believed he wasn't equipped with that most basic of human outlets. Now he knew. Among all the horrors he'd survived, *nothing* had hurt enough, mattered enough, to wring tears from his soul.

Her rejection far more than hurt. She far more than mattered.

He'd opened himself to her, let her in all the way. He'd let go of his safeguards, his anger, his pride. He'd believed in what he thought they shared. He'd deluded himself that she must have come to feel the same for him, to be that magnificent to him.

She felt nothing but abhorrence. She'd been forced into this marriage, hated bowing to the dictates of desire and the demands of patriotism. She despised him and loathed the idea of carrying his child.

He pushed away from the wall, slowly, methodically wiped away the unknown weakness, the manifestation of his surrender, his dependence. Then he headed back to Clarissa.

What she felt changed nothing. She was his wife. His queen. The mother of his child. What *he* felt didn't matter.

He'd lived without a heart until he'd seen her. He'd grown one to love her with. It had been quivering and dancing in hope within him since their first night together. And she'd stilled it forever in one annihilating blow. Now it was as good as nonexistent again. And he'd just have to learn to live without it again.

The first crushing wave of misery receded.

Clarissa knew it would only crash over her with more brutal force when it gathered momentum. For now, she was floating within the calm between devastating hurricanes. Now she could analyze her misery, not just come apart under its onslaught.

So she was pregnant. According to the doctors, she'd been pregnant for a while. Now that they'd explained the mystery of the period she'd had, she knew. She'd gotten pregnant that first night. As Ferruccio, in his endless insight, had foreseen she would. It was the best thing that had ever happened to her. It was by far the worst, too.

Now she'd never know if Ferruccio would remain married to her to have *her,* or to have his child. She'd been fooling herself, telling herself it wouldn't matter as long as he remained this wonderful to her. She *couldn't* live her life beside him, not knowing if he reciprocated her feelings, or knowing he couldn't. That day he'd struck his bargain, he'd said that if either of them wanted to be with someone else, they'd find a civil solution.

What if that bargain wasn't erased, and his heart was untouched? What if, one day, he found the woman to touch it?

She finally understood the depths of misery and desperation that had eaten through her mother's psyche, that had driven her, as they all suspected, to end her own life, when she'd come to believe that the husband she'd worshipped hadn't just never loved her, but had given his heart to another.

"Clarissa."

Ferruccio's whisper hit her all the way from the door, clanged inside her as if he'd shouted her name.

She jerked around, thanked God her tears had dried. Her lips trembled into a smile of dread and longing. What was he thinking?

His tranquil steps brought him to her side in what seemed like an eternity. Why was he so calm? So…opaque?

He sat down beside her on the bed, reached out a gentle hand and stroked away tendrils of hair from her face. The tenderness of his touch didn't match his guarded look. *Dio…Dio…*he wasn't happy about this. She knew it. Just before he'd been told the news, he'd been passionate, impatient, eager…open. Now it seemed that he'd retreated where she couldn't see him, let alone reach him.

Basta, you idiot! This was as life-changing to him as it was to her. He'd just been told he'd become a father for the first time. And to him, of all people, having a child within a solid, happy marriage, giving it what he'd never had, raising it between two loving parents, must be his foremost priority in life.

If their marriage was solid and happy.

"*Congratulazioni, futura mamma.*" She tried to sit up, throw herself in his arms. He stopped her. She almost started weeping again, at his care. That he didn't take her in his arms. "No, don't move. No more bouncing around, and no more work until the doctors say it's one thousand percent safe."

"As long as it's not no more you, I'm fine with it." She tried to quip, knew he must see the turmoil in her eyes. She saw nothing in his as he brushed her quivering lips with his own.

"We'll see about that. Now rest, Clarissa." He withdrew, and she felt as if he would never come back. He looked down at her for a long moment. Then he exhaled. "I have to get back to work, but anything you need, *amore,* just summon me. I'll bring the whole world to you."

But I just want you.

The cry congealed in her throat as he turned and walked away.

He'd said all the right things, was fussing over her health and comfort. But he hadn't said how he felt about this. Not that he needed to. She'd never seen him look despondent. Now she had.

So he didn't want a child that would tie him to her forever? But if he hadn't wanted it, why hadn't he used protection? Did he just want the baby to cement his claim to the D'Agostino family name, but would rather she didn't come attached to it?

Was this how her mother had gone mad, destroyed her life and attempted to destroy the child of the man who couldn't love her?

But no. She wasn't her mother. She was herself, and no matter that she felt she was dying inside, she'd live for her child, love it more because it was his, too.

Even if he never loved her, she would always love him.

Clarissa finished watering her plants, then sat down to leaf through the baby magazines Ferruccio had deluged her with.

She looked at all the dimpled, smiling babies and felt she was sinking soundlessly in quicksand. The more she struggled with the determination to make the best of it, the faster she sank.

"Clarissa."

The lethal growl jammed her heart into her throat. *Durante.*

She swung around, suddenly seething with anger. "*Maledizione,* Durante, why did you bark at me like that—?"

The words froze on her lips, followed by the blood in her arteries. He…he looked…rabid.

Had something happened? To their father? To Gabrielle and their baby? But no…he didn't look agitated, he looked incensed, murderous.

Suspicion bludgeoned her heart.

Ferruccio and Gabrielle…?

His next words confirmed her most insane paranoia. "I had to see you, tell you, before I killed them both."

She flew to him, threw herself at him. "Durante, *no*."

"Those two bastards deserve to die."

Two *bastards?* He was talking about two men? Ferruccio must be one of them. Who was the second? Gabrielle had more than one lover?

Could this get more insane?

Durante grabbed her arms. "You have to know how this happened. Before I married Gabrielle, I confronted our father, and he confessed he'd had a mistress for a very long time. I wanted to know the rest of the truth, but he wouldn't tell me, so I made investigations, found out his mistress was Gabrielle's mother. I went mad, drove Gabrielle away. *Grazie a Dio,* she took me back when I came to my senses and realized she had nothing to do with our parents' affair. But I forgot to call off my investigators. A few days ago their boss called with evidence that Gabrielle's mother had thirty-eight years ago given birth in Napoli to a son, then given him up for adoption. Along with the other evidence, the suspicion was too much. So I had DNA tests done. And redone. The results are conclusive. That son was Ferruccio. He is our father's son."

Eleven

How many times since Ferruccio had entered her life had he caused the world stop for her? Now it had stopped making sense, devolved into absolute chaos and madness.

Durante had said…had said…

Her mind shut down. Then Ferruccio walked in.

He stood at the door, his eyes moving from Durante to her in a slow sweep. Then they closed. He understood what this was all about. And since he did, then he'd…he'd known he was…was…

Ferruccio rushed to her, urgency blazing on his face, vibrating in his voice. "*Amore,* it is *not* what you think."

Durante slammed into him, aborting his momentum, wrestled him by the lapels, roared. "You don't talk to her, you bastard. Say whatever it is you want to say to me, before I kill you."

Clarissa noted, with the detachment of total breakdown, Ferruccio breaking Durante's hold with the explosive economy only a vicious, expert streetfighter could employ.

He staggered away, the turmoil on his face that of a man about to amputate his own arm. "I wanted to take this to my grave, but you've cornered me, Durante. I can't let either of you suspect what you do for one more second. I have to tell you the truth."

The truth. From the agony in his pleading eyes, it was something worse than anything that had come before. When there could be nothing worse. Yet it seemed there was. And he would finally tell her. Would she survive it? Would she want to?

Ferruccio knew the secrecy was over. He had to confess. It still felt like he was tearing out his own heart. Because he'd tear out Clarissa's with his confession. He would have given his heart for hers if it would have resolved this, protected her. But it wouldn't. There was no way out.

"Yes, I am the king's son." He panted with the effort of having to deal Clarissa such irreparable damage. Then he did. "It's you, Clarissa, who is not his daughter."

Clarissa collapsed.

His heart and skull felt as if they'd exploded.

He was beside her, catching her before she finished her plummet, frantically begging her to come back to him. He barely felt the vise that sank in his shoulder. Durante's grip.

"Is that the truth?"

He glared up at his half brother. "You think I'd lie about something like this? If you do, why don't you take a hair from her, too, and run more 'conclusive tests'?"

Durante seemed about to collapse himself. "*Dio*...what kind of parents did we have?"

"We still have one around. At least, you and I do. Both of Clarissa's are dead." Ferruccio carried Clarissa as if she were made of fragile glass, took her to their bedroom. She was breathing easy. Her nervous system must have shut down to protect her from any real damage. He still called his air ambulance and her doctors, told them to stand by.

He sat down beside her on their bed, which they hadn't shared for the past week. He'd been dying to have her, and he'd felt her equal need for him, but he hadn't been able to initiate intimacies. He'd done her enough damage, had wanted her to be the one to seek physical pleasure from him, at her own pace, of her own unpressured volition.

Now all he wanted was to curve himself around her and protect her from her pain and shock, beg her to take of him all she needed to heal herself.

"So you're my half brother. Why did you never tell me?"

Durante. He was still here.

Ferruccio turned to him, feeling worse than he had after a gang had broken almost every bone in his body.

"For her." Durante answered his own question. "You never wanted the truth about her parentage to become known, or for this terrible suspicion to stand in the way of your courting her."

"I've always wanted to tell you, but I loved her more. I was content that you thought of me as a friend."

"*Best* friend, Ferruccio. And now, brother."

"Yes. But, my best friend and brother, for now, please leave me alone with my wife."

Durante pressed his shoulder once, his eyes glittering with emotion, then he turned around.

When he was at the door, Ferruccio called out after him. "And leave King Benedetto alone."

Durante shook his head, gave a mirthless, ragged laugh. "Now, how did you know confronting him would be the first thing I'd do?"

"I'm serious, Durante. This must stay between us. I don't want King Benedetto learning that Clarissa has found out the truth. He spent his life protecting her from it. It would serve nothing but to make him desolate."

Durante closed his eyes on a grudging nod. "We have a lifetime and six years of acquaintance to rewrite."

"Actually, many lifetimes, Durante. Mine, your mother's, my mother's, Clarissa's father's. When and if I'm able to resolve this mess with my wife, if anything good comes of this, it will be that we finally forge a deeper relationship as siblings.

In secret. This *isn't* going public under any conditions. You'd better have been careful in your investigations."

"My investigator only came up with circumstantial evidence, he couldn't learn your identity. It's me who worked that out. I kept the medical evidence anonymous, the samples unnamed. Only I knew who they belonged to."

"Good. Now please, get out of here. Let me tend to my wife."

"You love her the way I love Gabrielle, don't you?" Durante's eyes filled with wonder, relief. "You would die for her."

"To start with. Now, get."

This time when he turned away, Durante did leave, still clearly in turmoil, but with a smile on his face.

Ferruccio forgot him the moment he exited his field of vision. He forgot that a world beyond the woman filling his arms existed. And he did what he'd longed to do for the past week.

He curved himself around her, contained her, whispered against her velvet cheek, "I'm here, *amore.* I'll always be here."

Clarissa surfaced from the nightmare, struggling to reach for the soothing lure reiterating, "I'm here. I'll always be here."

"I'm not who I thought I was."

Her own voice finally dragged her out of the vortex.

She'd passed out. To escape the medley of living nightmares she'd been living through. Living without Ferruccio's love, the horrible suspicion, then the terrible truth.

It had to be the truth. A DNA test like the one Durante had done would prove it. But she didn't need a test. She knew Ferruccio had told the truth. And he'd known it all this time.

He gathered her tighter to him. She didn't know if the tremors originated from her body or his arms.

"It doesn't matter. You remain the same, your life does, past and future. Your father…"

She whimpered.

"He *is* your father. He never cared that you aren't his biologically."

"He knew…all along?" Could this get worse? And she wailed, "How did this happen? Ferruccio, *please,* tell me the whole truth."

Every muscle in his face worked. Then he at last nodded.

"My mother's name was Clarisse LeFehr." At her gasp, he took her lips in a compulsive kiss. "Yes. *He* named you, Clarissa. He loved you from the moment you were born, and he named you for the love of his life. She was a ballerina with an Italian ballet company that performed in Castaldini. He was the new king, and they fell madly in love. Then she betrayed him, or so he believed. He cast her out of his life, immediately took a 'suitable' wife, your mother, Angelina. Their marriage was arranged, with no passion on either side. Even so, they had Durante, then Paolo. King Benedetto said he cared for her, but could never love her, not when he still loved his ex-lover, my mother. Then *your* mother's old lover—Pierro Bartolli, the man her father must have 'disciplined' her over—resurfaced, and she resumed their affair. When she got pregnant with you, she told him she would leave your father. But he convinced her not to, said that they would remain lovers. So she confessed to the king.

"At the same time, the king had long discovered that my mother hadn't betrayed him. Knowing how much he'd wronged her, and having never stopped loving her, he'd been searching for her, intent on resuming their relationship. So he felt as responsible as your mother for the situation. He told her they'd continue to project a façade of a solid marriage for their children's and their kingdom's sake, that he'd love her daughter as the daughter he'd longed to have.

"Your mother probably didn't believe him, and that may be why she overprotected you when you were young. But your biological father—according to King Benedetto—was only using her to live way beyond his means. When she'd expended all her personal fortune on him, Pierro tried to pressure her into asking the king for money, or even to steal it for him. He verbally abused her. She started pawning her jewelry for him, and Antonia told the king, who got it back and basically put your mother under house arrest. She considered him a jailer, escaped and went to her lover. She found him with another woman. When he was certain she couldn't get him more funds, he told her she was worth nothing without the money she'd provided him with from the first day, that he'd spent all her money on his lover, a woman she wasn't fit to be a servant to. I think that's when she began to abuse you."

"She wrote all that in her diaries. Durante thought she'd meant our…*his* father." She struggled to hold back sobs. Then she choked, "What happened to my…my biological father? Pierro? What about his…my…family."

Ferruccio's face became impassive. She guessed he was trying to withhold his opinion of the man who'd abused her mother and denied her, his flesh and blood. He didn't want to add to her turmoil. She felt rage and affront blasting off him. But when he spoke, he sounded controlled, neutral. "Pierro died five years ago, just before your mother did. In a boating accident. As far as I know, he had no living relatives. He came from a background much like my own."

"And his death…that was why she…" Her words choked off again, her tears now a stream.

But they weren't tears of pain or shock anymore. They were tears of pity. For the pettiness of it all, the waste. And of relief. The release of finally knowing how and why. Of closure.

Through her tears, she saw something she'd never thought to see. Tears in Ferruccio's eyes. *Those* hurt.

She surged up, clutched his face. "No, Ferruccio, no… please, don't cry. Not you."

"You suffered so much, *amore*. And now…"

"Now I'm just relieved I know at last." A tear escaped down his cheek and she cried out, caught it with her lips. "Don't make me hate myself for daring to feel devastated for a second, when I had the loving father—*your* father and the privileged upbringing, while you had *nothing*."

He wiped at his tears, his smile coming out a grimace that severed more of her heart's tethers. "I have everything now."

"That doesn't make it any better."

"It more than does. It erases it."

She felt she'd have a seizure from the pressure of her emotions. She wanted to scream and say that nothing would ever erase his suffering. That not even her and her father's lives would be enough to repay what they owed him. "Tell me the rest, Ferruccio. Your story. Did my…your father know about you, too?"

He looked away. She guessed that he didn't want to add to her pain. *Her* pain. Hatred, for herself, for her father, for the world, shot to a new height. She grabbed his face, forced him to look at her.

At last he muttered. "He found out when I was fifteen."

"And he left you on the streets? *Oh, Dio…Dio…*"

He sat up, taking her with him, cradling her in the curve of his body. "*Amore,* it doesn't matter."

"*Doesn't matter?* That is the worst thing yet. It's unbearable. Unimaginable. It's an unforgivable crime!"

"It didn't happen like you think."

"Then tell me how it did happen before my head bursts!"

He exhaled his surrender to her need to know. "When King Benedetto sought out my mother, she was married, and she'd already had Gabrielle."

It clicked in her mind. "Gabrielle is your sister! *That's* why you look at her that way!"

"Yes. I thought I'd never be able to approach her, since the price was telling her the truth. Even with Durante's prior investigations and the subsequent revelations before she married him, she remained ignorant she had a brother."

"But even without knowing, she…recognized the bond between you. I can swear she did."

"It was fun to see you act jealous, though. It gave me hope."

She wasn't in a condition to understand what that meant.

"And you were willing to live your whole life not telling her that you are brother and sister, to protect me from the truth?"

"Considering I have her in my life anyway, that isn't such a huge sacrifice."

"*Dio,* Ferruccio, shut up. And *talk.*"

He huffed a distressed laugh. "I said exactly that to your doctors a week ago. And if you're in half as appalling a state as I was then, I'd better talk fast. Just promise me, no more tears."

Her eyes gushed again. "No can do. Please, Ferruccio. You were saying your mother was married, had Gabrielle…?"

He kept wiping her tears with his fingers, his lips. "When King Benedetto reappeared in her life, she told him about me, how in her worst moments after she'd given birth, she'd weakened and put me up for adoption. She tried to look for me later, to take me back, but she'd been denied information. All she could find out was that I was never adopted, that I ended up in the foster system. They searched for me, but didn't find me until two years after I left my last foster home. They were heartbroken to find their son a hardened survivor on the streets."

"*They* were heartbroken? The nerve!"

"There was no villain here, *amore,* it was all a series of horrible miscommunications and terrible decisions."

"Which *are* crimes, and makes them villains, especially since there was only one victim. You!"

"Are you defending me again, *leonessa mia?* Against the pain of the past and the mistakes of my parents?"

"If that pain and those mistakes were flesh and blood now, I'd tear them apart with my teeth and nails!"

His laugh was delighted this time, as he hugged her. "You see? Hearing you say that erases it all." An impatient, indignant sound rolled from her throat. He raised a placating hand. "Don't growl, *leonessa mia.* I'll go on peacefully."

He adjusted their position to place her on his lap, where she could feel every rock-hard inch of him thrusting between her legs. Even through the upheaval, her body blossomed and melted into instant readiness. How she'd starved for him.

"My parents were justifiably shocked. I was a hulking, surly, violent teenager they had every reason to suspect would become, or already was, a hardened criminal."

"Thanks to them!"

"Actually, I don't believe there is any excuse for turning to crime. Not neglect, not hardships, not abuse. I never considered my ordeals a reason to take the easy way out."

"I did tell you before, Ferruccio. You are a miracle."

"Look who's talking." He hugged her again, pressed his forehead to hers in a gesture that melted all her heart valves. "But I did look scary. And as much as they were shocked to see me, I was shocked to see them, to discover that I wasn't just any bastard, but a royal one. The king pledged to support me, but he told me, for the sake of his family and kingdom, he wouldn't be able to acknowledge me. I told him what to do with his support. The only thing I'd ever accept from him was his name."

"He's the man who raised me, and I love him. But I also hate him now. How could he think his other children more important than you? How could he deny you what he gave them?"

"It was all for you, *mia bella unica.* He might have lost you completely if a chain reaction of revelations was started."

To that she could only sob and bury her face in his chest. She tugged at him to go on.

"The king kept putting money for me in the bank, enough to have seen me through a luxurious life and the best education."

She glanced up. "But you never touched it."

His chuckle rumbled beneath her ear. "You know me well. That money in the bank was like a tormenting imp, lashing me to succeed, to reach ever higher on my own. I was bent on showing him I didn't need him in any way. So, I guess I should thank him for that. And because I became who I am, I can now do all I'm doing for Castaldini. So in a roundabout way, all of Castaldini is in your father's debt, too."

"In his debt for not acknowledging his son?" she seethed. "Excuse me as I puke! And bull to this owing your success to your ordeals or to anyone. You would have suceeded no matter what!"

"But maybe I wouldn't have become the same man."

The man I worship? she almost blurted out.

She didn't. It was time she asked the question that really mattered to her. "T-tell me about the first time you came to Castaldini."

"Ah, that first time. Even with my very…eventful life, that was the day its course changed forever." The look he gave her told her she'd been the reason.

How?

"With my success established and the fire in my heart banked, I felt the need to establish some sort of relationship with the king. So I came here on the pretext of doing business. The king was ecstatic that I'd decided to come to him at last. I even felt that he'd finally acknowledge me, that everything was going right. Then I saw you."

She clutched at his shirt, which she'd soaked in tears. She sensed that she'd now hear what would explain the past—and unravel the future.

"I'd never wanted anyone on sight like that. And I thought I saw the same recognition, the same instant hunger in your eyes. But before I could walk up to you and claim you, the king joined me and something he said made me realize that you were his daughter. I was so appalled that I walked away without looking at him. I think I would have decked him if I hadn't."

That was it. The mystery behind the misery that had ruled her for the past six years. Everything fell into place like a hail of bombs. "And you reached for the first woman—or two—to drown your sorrow."

His gaze stilled before he threw his head back and barked a stunned laugh. "*Maledizione,* you're uncanny, *mia bella.* I was out to prove to myself there were plenty of other fish in the sea." His lips twisted wryly. "And the moment I felt my sinker bob,

I tossed the whole fishing rod into the water and ran away. And that was when the king found me again, dragged me away. The minute we were alone, I turned on him, ranting that I hated him, that he was the reason for every horrible thing that had ever happened to me and that I'd never come back.

"But he understood the reason behind my turmoil. He'd seen the hunger in my eyes as I looked at you, said he was stunned at the clarity of instinct that had told me I could covet you. And he told me the secret he'd intended to take to his grave—that you weren't his biological child. He'd decided by then to make my parentage known, to let you and the world believe that I was your half brother. I refused point-blank, and he said that meant he'd have to let the truth about *your* parentage be known.

"And I made my decision. I would remain the illegitimate one among us. I was used to it, and it meant nothing to me anymore. While you—I couldn't bear to think of your devastation if you found out the king wasn't your father."

She heaved a huge sob and burst out weeping again. He stroked and soothed her. "It was in my best interests. As a stranger, I was free to pursue you. When I said that, the king was alarmed, said he wouldn't let me toy with you. I said he had no say in the matter, but should put his mind to rest, anyway. That clarity of instinct he'd talked about had always made me sure of what I wanted, what would work, and work spectacularly. And I'd never been surer about anything. I wanted you. And I was getting you. And it would be beyond spectacular."

Her tears stopped, foreboding squeezing her heart. He'd come to the part when she'd smacked his advances back in his face.

"But I shouldn't have been so sure. I went after you, and you turned me down, so disdainfully. Kept on doing it for six years. It took a crisis in your kingdom and some convoluted blackmail to make you accept me."

Suddenly his body stiffened beneath her, his jaw muscles

bunched as if in excruciating pain. Then he carefully set her away from him, rose to his feet, a defeated slump to his shoulders. "Not that you have accepted me."

Clarissa lay on the bed where he left her, pinned under a mountain of humility and gratitude and love and awe.

Then her mind caught on this last comment, and she was on her feet, across the room and grabbing him by the arms. "I work with you by day and make delirious love with you every night—at least, before you suddenly seemed to stop wanting me after you found out I was carrying your child. What do you *mean* I haven't accepted you?"

Ferruccio looked down at her, his reason and reasons made flesh and bone, his soul made woman. And he let his anguish out. "I mean you're trapped in our marriage. You don't want my child, you've always believed I'm beneath you. That was always the reason, from that first night, that you rejected me, wasn't it?"

She gaped at him. Then she started shaking him with all her strength. "Are you *really* insane? *Beneath* me? You thought my rejection all these years was rooted in snobbery? How dare you think me that stupid and vicious and shallow. How dare you want me when you thought that of me."

"I didn't…" He stopped, swallowed the knot of confusion that had never let him finish a coherent thought in this matter. "I did think that. But then I was with you, and everything you said and did told me you were everything I could admire and love. Then you rejected me *again,* and I could find no other explanation. I was going around and around in my mind, on an endless spin cycle of belief and doubt, hope and despair."

"*Dio,* this is beyond ridiculous. It seems you're not all-seeing, after all. Not with a blind spot the size of Africa."

"So, why did you keep rejecting me?" he groaned.

And she yelled at him, at the top of her voice, telling him exactly why she'd been scared to give in to him, to her feelings.

He was shaking with relief and elation when she finished.

But she wasn't finished. "And just what were *you* feeling all the time, as you thought that of me? Were you internally gloating at the stupid snob who was herself illegitimate? If so, I wonder at your willpower that you haven't smeared my face in it. But then, you should have. Maybe then you would have gotten your facts straight, and all this could have been resolved earlier."

He opened his mouth to protest and she bulldozed on. "And don't you dare turn this on me. It's you who seem to be trapped in our marriage, you who are unhappy that I'm carrying your baby. The day you found out, you looked as if you'd been told you had a chronic, debilitating disease."

He was shaking as hard as she was now, finally seeing it all. "I saw you crying. I went back to thinking you hated me, couldn't stand having my baby. *Dio santo,* Clarissa, we've both been so afraid to believe all this magic was for real that we kept tormenting ourselves with worst-case scenarios."

Her violet eyes turned purple with the enormity of emotion igniting them, the silvery tears magnifying their beauty, reflecting shards of pure, agonizing ecstasy into his soul.

"So do you want my baby? And…me?" Then he added the word he'd held back during their marriage ceremony. "Forever?"

She dove into his arms, felt as if she surged into his being, as she had—lived there now, ruled supreme. "Since I love you endlessly, you'd better make it at least that long."

He held her tight, then tighter, and they exchanged confessions and pledges and he soothed her turmoil over her discoveries, wallowed in the still wary, yet deepening certainty of their mutual devotion.

When it all threatened to overwhelm them again, and fearing for her health, both emotional and physical, he suddenly tickled her.

"Now I am the king's bastard and the bastard king. While you are the queen's bastard and the bastard queen. How's that for proof we're made for each other?"

She kissed him, sobbed and giggled. "*Uomo cattivo,* you wicked man, how dare you make it funny when it isn't?"

"No, it isn't. But it's destiny. Ours."

"Show me."

He swept her into his arms and showed her. And with every word and touch, he wrote with her another page in what he was now certain was a destiny that would leave its mark on the world.

Epilogue

Ferrucio looked around the room where his family had gathered.

He still couldn't believe it. He still woke up suffocating, fearing that the last twenty-one months hadn't happened. That he was alone, with only work for company and comfort.

Each time, he'd woken up in Clarissa's arms. Which made him fear even more that he was dreaming.

But he couldn't have dreamed her. His wildest imaginings wouldn't have created her, his wife and best friend and ally, his queen and lover. And as if she wasn't beyond what any mortal deserved, she'd gifted him with more.

Their son.

His heart almost burst yet again, as he watched their determined tyke trying in vain to catch Clarissa's disdainful—and he suspected, intentionally taunting—cat, Figaro. Love and pride and fear and hope reduced his insides to the consistency of jelly.

It was a whole year today, since their perfect Massimo was

born. And the months before he was born had all flowered in escalating harmony and pleasure and joy.

It wasn't just his and Clarissa's tiny family that was flourishing. The king—or the ex-king, as he insisted on being called, an insistence which no one heeded—was in the best condition he'd been in since his stroke. Julia, Phoebe's sister, was in the best state she'd ever been in since her affliction with a rare partial paralysis. Gabrielle and Durante, after their initial confusion, were delighted to share Ferruccio as a sibling, Gabrielle on her mother's side, Durante on his father's. While Durante's and Paolo's relationship with Clarissa seemed only to deepen, now that the real cause behind their mother's depression had come to light.

"Admiring the view?"

Ferruccio turned to see Leandro. Durante was a step behind. He greeted his two friends, whom he'd finally been able to tell they were more than that and whom it had taken minimal groveling to get to become his main men on the new Council they'd forged, the one Castaldini needed now.

"What's not to admire?" Ferruccio said. "Look at her. Have you ever seen anything more miraculous?"

"Uh, actually, yes." Leandro smirked. "Take a look around."

Ferruccio did, this time attempting to focus on anyone besides Clarissa and Massimo. Phoebe was at her most radiant, talking animatedly to Julia and Gabrielle and the king. Her and Leandro's little girl, Joia, now twenty months old, was fast asleep on Phoebe's round-again tummy. Gabrielle and Durante's fourteen-month-old boy, Alessandro, was playing with the fifth—and they swore last—addition to Paolo and Julia's family, with their older kids all over the place yet managing not to be noisy or disruptive, mostly babysitting the younger ones to give adults space to talk.

Durante nodded. "We're all lucky bastards."

"Since I'm the literal lucky bastard among you," Ferruccio said, "I reserve my place as the luckiest among us."

"Let him have first place, Durante." Leandro smirked. "He just can't live if he isn't the first in everything."

Ferruccio started to protest, then shook his head and laughed. He *was* the luckiest. No need to rub their noses in it.

The other two men joined him in laughter.

Clarissa scooped Massimo off the ground before he grabbed Figaro's tail. Figaro knew he was a kid, treated him with the condescending tolerance the status deserved. But the imperious tomcat had his limits. His tail was foremost among them.

She turned around at the sound of three men's laughter, her heart twisting with love as she watched her *amore,* her king and husband. She hadn't thought she could possibly love him more, but she did, every day. For who he was, what he did, not only for her, but for all of Castaldini, the kingdom that was once again a haven of peace and prosperity. But one thing made her so grateful to him, so proud of him, she sometimes couldn't breathe, thinking of it.

The incredible sacrifice he'd so selflessly insisted on, to remain the "bastard king," as he called himself, to protect his father and her. They'd never let King Benedetto suspect that she knew the truth. She loved him now even more, for being her father when he wasn't her real father. She felt his eyes on her now.

She walked up to him and whispered in his ear. He nodded.

"Hey, everyone!" she called out, and everyone turned to her, a hush falling over the huge chamber. "King Benedetto—hush, Father—" she shushed him when he protested to being called king now, as he never failed to "—has some news for you!"

As everyone turned to him, all attention, he stood up and took his first steps since Ferruccio's and Clarissa's wedding. Strong steps, almost with no visible limp. He'd been practicing, exercising, but hadn't wanted anyone to know until he was able to walk without his cane. He'd told only her.

The chamber echoed with sounds of delight as everyone surged to congratulate him.

Ferruccio was the last to approach.

Clarissa's heart ached. Ferruccio still considered King Benedetto her father, not his, and the tension in their relationship was not completely gone. He said he loved the king for being her father, for protecting her as a child, for loving her as she deserved to be loved. She still prayed for the day he'd come to love him for himself, to forgive him his trespasses and guilt.

Now the considering look Ferruccio gave her father rattled her with anxiety. He'd never say anything cutting to him, not anymore, especially not now. But what did that look mean?

Ferruccio stood before her father, seemed to be examining him. Then he said, "Seems to me you're back in tip-top shape. Does this mean you want the crown back?"

She exhaled her immense relief at his obvious teasing, as King Benedetto embraced him.

Ferruccio stepped back from his father's embrace, doing a double take. What was that he saw on the old jackal's face? That smug, got-you-where-I-want-you look?

He didn't have time to interrogate him, as the women and children swept the king away. Ferruccio turned to Leandro and Durante, saw the same puzzled look on their faces.

"Tell me you saw that," Durante exclaimed.

"I saw it." Leandro nodded. "I think he meant for us to see it."

"Dio," Ferruccio groaned. "I feel like the biggest sucker in the known universe."

"Oh no you don't." Duranted echoed his groan. "That is one status you'll have to share with us."

"This was all a plan. A master plan by your canny old man." Leandro shook his head in wonder, admiration tingeing his gaze as he looked at King Benedetto.

"Everything falls into place, doesn't it? We're all exactly where he wanted us to be all along," Ferruccio said.

The three of them exchanged looks, suspicion becoming conviction in a heartbeat.

They all burst out laughing at the same moment.

"For the first time in my life," Ferruccio guffawed, "I want to kiss the man. I want to smother him in kisses."

"You'll have to wait in line." Durante wiped away tears of hilarity.

Leandro still shook his head, the look of admiration on his face deepening. "Between our hugs and kisses of overwhelming gratitude, we might even make him sorry for manipulating us so unrepentantly."

"And considering what we all ended up having," Ferruccio said fervently, "*grazie a Dio* a billion times that he did."

"Amen, *fratello*, amen." Durante echoed his passion.

At that moment Clarissa walked up to Ferruccio.

He scooped her off the ground into a convulsive hug. She giggled and hugged him back, whispered in his ear.

He froze before he whooped and swung her into the air.

As everyone gaped at them, he clutched her in his arms and rushed out on a beeline to their apartments.

He couldn't have waited to make an announcement out of her news.

Having a second baby on the way was something he needed to celebrate in private first, and urgently.

* * * * *

Celebrate 60 years of pure reading pleasure with Harlequin!

To commemorate the event, Harlequin Intrigue® is thrilled to invite you to the wedding of The Colby Agency's J. T. Baxley and his bride, Eve Mattson.

That is, of course, if J.T. can find the woman who left him at the altar. Considering he's a private investigator for one of the top agencies in the country—the best of the best—that shouldn't be a problem. The real setback is that his bride isn't who she appears to be...and her mysterious past has put them both in danger.

Enjoy an exclusive glimpse of Debra Webb's latest addition to
THE COLBY AGENCY: ELITE RECONNAISSANCE DIVISION

THE BRIDE'S SECRETS

Available August 2009 from Harlequin Intrigue®.

The dark figures on the dock were still firing. The bullets cutting through the surface of the water without the warning boom of shots told Eve they were using silencers.

That was to her benefit. Silencers decreased the accuracy of every shot and lessened the range.

She grabbed for the rocks. Scrambled through the darkness. Bumped her knee on a boulder. Cursed.

Burrowing into the waist-deep grass, she kept low and crawled forward. Faster. Pushed harder. Needed as much distance as possible.

Shots pinged on the rocks.

J.T. scrambled alongside her.

He was breathing hard.

They had to stay close to the ground until they reached the next row of warehouses. Even though she was relatively certain they were out of range at this point, she wasn't taking any risks. And she wasn't slowing down.

J.T. had to keep up.

The splat of a bullet hitting the ground next to Eve had her rolling left. Maybe they weren't completely out of range.

She bumped J.T. He grunted.

His injured arm. Dammit. She could apologize later.

Half a dozen more yards.

Almost in the clear.

As she reached the cover of the alley between the first two warehouses she tensed.

Silence.

No pings or splats.

She glanced back at the dock. Deserted.

Time to run.

Her car was parked another block down.

Pushing to her feet, she sprinted forward. The wet bag dragged at her shoulder. She ignored it.

By the time she reached the lot where her car was parked, she had dug the keys from her pocket and hit the fob. Six seconds later she was behind the wheel. She hit the ignition as J.T. collapsed into the passenger seat. Tires squealed as she spun out of the slot.

"What the hell did you do to me?"

From the corner of her eye she watched him shake his head in an attempt to clear it.

He would be pissed when she told him about the tranquilizer.

She'd needed him cooperative until she formulated a plan. A drug-induced state of unconsciousness had been the fastest and most efficient method to ensure his continued solidarity.

"I can't really talk right now." Eve weaved into the right lane as the street widened to four lanes. What she needed was traffic. It was Saturday night—shouldn't be that difficult to find as soon as they were out of the old warehouse district.

A glance in the rearview mirror warned that their unwanted company had caught up.

Sensing her tension, J.T. turned to peer over his left shoulder. "I hope you have a plan B."

She shot him a look. "There's always plan G." Then she pulled the Glock out of her waistband.

Cutting the steering wheel left, she slid between two vehicles. Another veer to the right and she'd put several cars between hers and the enemy.

She was betting they wouldn't pull out the firepower in the open like this, but a girl could never be too sure when it came to an unknown enemy.

Deep blending was the way to go.

Two traffic lights ahead the marquis of a movie theater provided exactly the opportunity she was looking for.

The digital numbers on the dash indicated it was just past midnight. Perfect timing. The late movie would be purging its audience into the crowd of teenagers who liked hanging out in the parking lot.

She took a hard right onto the property that sported a twelve-screen theater, numerous fast-food hot spots and a chain super-store. Speeding across the lot, she selected a lane of parking slots. Pulling in as close to the theater entrance as possible, she shut off the engine and reached for her door.

"Let's go."

Thankfully he didn't argue.

Rounding the hood of her car, she shoved the Glock into her bag, then wrapped her arm around J.T.'s and merged into the crowd.

With her free hand she finger-combed her long hair. It was soaked, as were her clothes. The kids she bumped into noticed, gave her death-ray glares.

They just didn't know.

As she and J.T. moved in closer to the building, she grabbed a baseball cap from an innocent bystander. The crowd made it easy. The kid who owned the cap had made it even easier by stuffing the cap bill-first into his waistband at the small of his back.

Pushing through the loitering crowd, she made her way to the side of the building next to the main entrance. She pushed

J.T. against the wall and dropped her bag to the ground. Peeled off her tee and let it fall.

His gaze instantly zeroed in on her breasts, where the cami she wore had glued to her skin like an extra layer. A zing of desire shot through her veins.

Not the time.

With a flick of her wrist she twisted her hair up and clamped the cap atop the blond mass.

"They're coming," J.T. muttered as he gazed at some point beyond her.

"Yeah, I know." She planted her palms against the wall on either side of him and leaned in. "Keep your eyes open. Let me know when they're inside."

Then she planted her lips on his.

* * * * *

Will J.T. and Eve be caught in the moment?
Or will Eve get the chance to reveal all of her secrets?
Find out in
THE BRIDE'S SECRETS
by Debra Webb
Available August 2009
from Harlequin Intrigue®

In 2009 Harlequin celebrates 60 years of pure reading pleasure!

We're marking this occasion by offering 16 **FREE** full books to download and read.

Visit

www.HarlequinCelebrates.com

to choose from a variety of great romance stories that are absolutely **FREE!**

(Total approximate retail value of $60)

We invite you to visit and share the Web site with your friends, family and anyone who enjoys reading.

SMP60WEB1

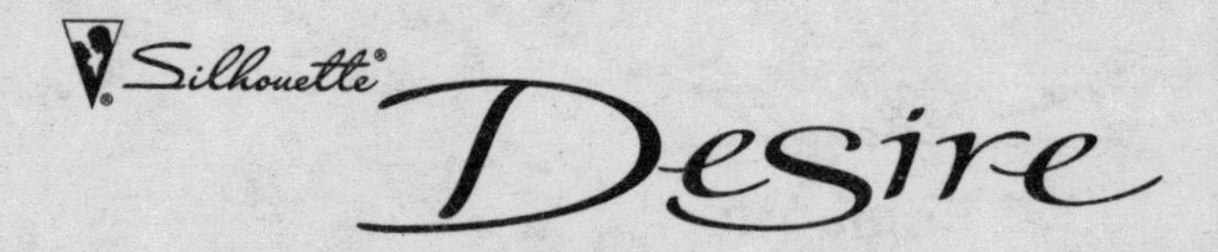

COMING NEXT MONTH

Available August 11, 2009

#1957 BOSSMAN BILLIONAIRE—Kathie DeNosky
Man of the Month
The wealthy businessman needs an heir. His plan: hire his attractive assistant as a surrogate mother. Her condition: marriage.

#1958 ONE NIGHT WITH THE WEALTHY RANCHER—Brenda Jackson
Texas Cattleman's Club: Maverick County Millionaires
Unable to deny the lingering sparks with the woman he once rescued, he's still determined to keep his distance…until her life is once again in danger.

#1959 SHEIKH'S BETRAYAL—Alexandra Sellers
Sons of the Desert
Suspicious of his former lover's true motives, the sheikh sets out to discover what brought her back to the desert. But soon it's unclear who's seducing whom….

#1960 THE TYCOON'S SECRET AFFAIR—Maya Banks
The Anetakis Tycoons
A surprise pregnancy is not what this tycoon had in mind after one blistering night of passion. Yet he insists on marrying his former assistant…until a paternity test changes everything.

#1961 BILLION-DOLLAR BABY BARGAIN—Tessa Radley
Billionaires and Babies
Suddenly co-guardians of an orphaned baby, they disliked each other from the start. Until their marriage of convenience flares with attraction impossible to deny….

#1962 THE MAGNATE'S BABY PROMISE—Paula Roe
This eligible bachelor must marry and produce an heir to keep the family business. So when he discovers a one-night stand is pregnant, nothing will get in his way of claiming the baby—and the woman—as his own.

SDCNMBPA0709